Written by
Tsukasa Mikuni

Illustrated by
YukiKana

Of Dragons and Fae

Is a Fairy Tale Ending Possible for the Princess's Hairstylist?

Cross
Infinite
World

Of Dragons and Fae: Is a Fairy Tale Ending Possible for the Princess's Hairstylist?!
Tsukasa Mikuni

Translation by Molly Lee

Illustration by YukiKana
Title Design by KC Fabellon
Editing by Yvonne Yeung and A.M. Perrone
Proofreading by Charis Messier and A.M. Perrone

This book is a work of fiction. Names, characters, businesses, places, events and incidents are either the products of the author's imagination or used in a fictitious manner. Any resemblance to actual events, locales, or persons, living or dead, is purely coincidental.

Of Dragons and Fae: Is a Fairy Tale Ending Possible for the Princess's Hairstylist?!
© 2018 by Tsukasa Mikuni
First published in Japan in 2019 by
Shufu to Seikatsu Sha CO.,LTD.
English translation rights reserved by
Cross Infinite World.

English translation ©2019 Cross Infinite World

Cross Infinite World
contact@crossinfworld.com
www.crossinfworld.com

Published in the United States of America

Visit us at www.crossinfworld.com
Facebook.com/crossinfworld
Twitter.com/crossinfworld
crossinfiniteworld.tumblr.com

First Digital Edition: November 2019
First Print Edition: July 2020

ISBN-13: 978-1-945341-39-7

TABLE OF CONTENTS

Chapter 1: The Stylist Gets Dumped

MY name is Mayna Spring, and I am a hairstylist. Contrary to what the name suggests, however, we do much more than simply *style* hair—we trim it, maintain proper grooming, choose hairstyles to suit a given client, and more.

Personally, I'm proud of the work I do. It's fulfilling, and I love it. But when it comes to most other things—romance included—I can't say I'm interested.

Or at least, I wasn't... until five days ago, when I met a man at the royal banquet who changed my perspective ever so slightly.

"At last, I've found you. You're my Bondmate," he said to me, his eyes glistening.

His name was Ray Alide, and he was a Dragonkin. He was a knight from the neighboring kingdom of Vaxwald, the land of dragons, and he was in attendance as the Prince's bodyguard.

"What's a Bondmate?" I asked.

"For a Dragonkin, it is our destined partner. A soulmate," he explained with a radiant smile.

"O-Oh my," I stammered bashfully.

The sudden confession caught me off guard, but I admit, I swooned a little. With blond hair, golden eyes, and an amicable personality I never would have expected from a Dragonkin, Ray seemed almost like a handsome prince from a fairy tale. And although I was a grown woman of twenty years, I had absolutely no prior experience and, quite frankly, was in over my head.

My parents ran a local barbershop, so I grew up learning about hair care from an early age. Then, just two years ago, I was chosen to serve as the personal hairstylist for the Princess of our great nation of Myulan. Since then, I've found myself far too busy to go on dates or deal with anything of the sort.

"Not to say that all Dragonkin have a predetermined Bondmate, mind you. Quite the opposite, in fact. The vast majority of us learn about love the same way your people do: through trial and error. But for those who are privileged to have a Bondmate, it is a tremendous blessing," Ray explained, smiling as though he could scarcely contain his joy.

"That's fascinating," I replied, "but... I mean, I don't know anything about you... and I'm not even nobility or anything! The only reason I'm at this banquet is because Princess Patricia wanted me to be on standby in case of a hair emergency. I'm her personal stylist, you see."

Granted, I certainly looked the part; I was wearing a suitably formal dress, with my perfectly maintained raven locks elaborately coiffed for the occasion. Ultimately, however, I was a mere commoner.

"Oh, that doesn't bother me. I may be Vaxwald nobility by birth, but to me, one's social status hardly matters," he answered without hesitation. After a moment, he furrowed his brows. "That said, this conversation probably should have waited until *after* I introduced myself, now that I think of it. I've gotten ahead of myself completely... I hope you can forgive my lack of discretion."

Though he was clearly elated to have found his one true Bondmate, he possessed the wherewithal to prioritize my feelings, something I appreciated. The two of us took a step back and introduced ourselves, with Ray conducting himself like the perfect gentleman. It was clear he was making an effort not to keep harping on about the Bondmate thing, lest I feel pressured.

Then, three days after the banquet:

"You're going back to Vaxwald the day after tomorrow, right?" I asked.

During his stay at the Myulan Castle, Ray had consistently found time in his schedule to come and visit me, and it was around this point that I had started to grow attached to his presence.

"Yes, I'll be returning with His Highness Prince Dario. Not to worry—I promise I'll write you letters, and I'll come see you whenever I can. We can take it slow, and if I someday win your heart, I hope you'll consider visiting me in Vaxwald, even if it's years from now." He paused, then added, "Honestly, I'm half-tempted to skip the wait and take you home with me right now."

The way he said it, I wasn't entirely sure he was joking.

As things stood, I was honored to be the sole stylist in attendance to the Princess of Myulan, and I wasn't eager to give that up just yet. However, I didn't see the harm in visiting Vaxwald someday, as Ray had suggested. I was curious to see what hairstyles were in fashion among Dragonkin women, and I wasn't opposed to the idea of opening my own salon there someday… with Ray at my side...

Looking back, I was stupid to even *consider* planning my life around some guy I had only known for three days. But love is blind, as they say, and first love all the more so.

On the day Ray was scheduled to leave Myulan, his attitude toward me drastically changed.

When I went to say goodbye and see him off, he turned to me with a frown and clipped out, "I'm sorry, but I need you to forget everything that happened between us over the past few days. It turns out you're not actually my Bondmate."

"What?" The almost icy look in his eyes made me recoil slightly. "I'm not your Bondmate?"

"Yes, it would appear I was mistaken."

His tone was too casual for someone who had previously struck me as dutiful and steadfast—someone who, twenty-four hours prior, had gazed at me with eyes that said I was his whole world. I could scarcely believe it. All the romance between us seemed to evaporate, just like that.

"I admit, I'm obviously not a Dragonkin, so I don't have all the details, but… is that even possible?"

"Again, I'm sorry for the misunderstanding I've caused, but the fact of the matter is, I made a mistake. I no longer feel any attraction to you, and I must ask that you forget whatever feelings you may have had for me. This is farewell, Mayna."

And with that, he climbed astride his horse, joined up with Prince Dario and the other knights, and rode off.

Meanwhile, I was left standing there, staring blankly after him. "What?" I said in a tiny voice. "Forget my feelings? Where did this even come from?"

First he drops all this "Bondmate" stuff on me, then he wins me over, and now this? It felt like a rude awakening from what was once a happy dream.

As the Dragonkin riders slowly shrank into the distance, I simply stood there, my fists shaking with formless rage—not at Ray, but myself. *How could I have been so stupid? I always told myself I'd never let a man pull one over on me like that. Why did I let myself get so carried away?*

I grit my teeth in frustration. Apparently, I was a lot more gullible than I realized.

"I guess I should be grateful this happened before things got serious... Maybe I'll just chalk it up to experience..." I grumbled to myself.

Just then, Princess Patricia wandered over with her attendants. Similar to myself and Ray, she had come to bid farewell to Prince Dario.

"If they can morph into dragons, then why don't they just fly home? Don't you find it silly, Mayna?" she asked me, wearing a sweet, almost cherubic expression befitting her sixteen years.

"Indeed," I replied halfheartedly.

"His Highness complimented me on my hair again today. He said my plaits were 'quite beautiful'! And it's all thanks to you!"

"I'm glad."

"He was *ever* so surprised to learn I have my very own personal stylist! Of course, surely even nobility would think it decadent, or so I imagine. After all, most simply ask a servant to handle it."

"Our profession is still somewhat of a novelty. Yes, I need to work harder... No more wasting time on romance..."

"Mayna? Are you all right? You seem a bit gloomy..." She blinked for a moment, then clapped her hands together. "I've got it! You must be sad to part with that fair-haired knight, aren't you? He did call you his Bondmate, after all. And you looked rather happy about it, I must say!"

"L-Let's not go there..." I was ashamed to think of how giddy and carefree I had been.

Reluctantly, I explained to Her Highness about how Ray had changed his tune.

"A *mistake*?" she repeated, eyes wide, brows furrowed in puzzlement. Meanwhile, her three attendants snickered to themselves, likely pleased to know the handsome knight had lost all interest in a *lowly hairstylist* such as myself. After all, his undivided attention had warranted a fair bit of envy in my direction.

I wasn't bothered by their scorn, however. Personally, I was ready to wash my hands of the entire affair.

"I'm just going to devote the rest of my life to my work... I never should've wasted my time on a man when I still have so much training ahead of me... From now on, my heart and soul belong to hair and hair alone... It's for the best..." I muttered dispassionately, my shoulders slumped, misery radiating from every inch of my being.

"Why, you look utterly crushed! Poor dear... Are you quite sure you're all right?" She frowned, her tone sympathetic. Even her attendants seemed to pity me.

There was no need, of course. My job was my whole life's purpose. Only my career could bring me true happiness.

...You believe me, right?

Chapter 2: Flowerfolk

EACH morning I start my day by getting ready. Naturally, as a hairstylist, this involves making sure my hair is on point—but here in Myulan, you don't have to work with hair to care about it. In our culture, women are expected to grow their hair out and wear it braided or tied up. And heaven help you if you're seen in public with your hair down—nothing could be more shameful.

For commoner ladies without rank or title, we aren't obligated to invest too much time into our hairstyle, probably because we don't generally *have* the time to spare. We can just throw it into a bun and forget about it.

"What should I do with my hair today...?" I murmured to myself as I stood before the mirror. My long ebony locks hung past my breasts, glossy from my daily haircare regimen, the tips curled inward naturally. For me, my hair was my pride and joy.

"I'll braid it into a side bun," I decided aloud, then quickly got to work.

First, I left my bangs down. Next, I styled a headband braid over them. An ordinary bun would give me a stiff, no-nonsense image, which was not what I wanted today. Instead, I took the rest of my hair and twisted it into a loose three-strand braid starting at the crown of my head, then tugged on each section to fan it out. Lastly, I gathered my hair just behind my right ear and pinned it into a messy bun.

Then it was time for the finishing touch: a hair ornament. Today I went with a silver butterfly, positioned just atop the bun. Embedded in its wings were turquoise stones, mimicking the plate-like patterns of a real butterfly. Nothing quite as fancy as jewels, of course, but it matched the color of my eyes; such was how I chose almost all of my hair ornaments. After all, if it matched my hair, it wouldn't stand out—thus, it was more effective to match it to my eyes or my dress instead.

"Perfect. Now it's time for another day of hard work."

Less than twenty-four hours ago I was dumped in spectacular fashion, and yet I found myself smiling. A cute hairstyle never failed to put me in a good mood; plus, my feelings for Ray had already faded. I had only known the man for five days—nowhere near long enough to constitute a full-scale "heartbreak." In the end, all it took was one night to cry it out, and then I was over him. *Really glad this mess happened before I fell for him completely.*

"Time to go see Her Highness."

And so I left my quarters and headed off to meet up with my client, the Princess.

"GOOD morning, Your Highness."

"Good morning, Mayna!"

When I arrived, Her Highness Princess Patricia was already wearing a small amount of makeup carefully applied by her other servants. Now it was my turn to style her hair. Then, once she was dressed, she would be ready for the public eye.

"Any special requests today?" I asked.

"Nope! Just surprise me like you always do."

She was still in her nightgown. I walked up and gently pulled her light blonde strands free of their constraints, letting them hang naturally to her posterior. Hair of this length could be accidentally damaged during sleep, resulting in painful breakage. Hence, we always put her hair up in braids just prior to bedtime.

I watched the other servants as they set about selecting her clothes and accessories for the day. This would serve as my inspiration for her hairstyle.

"Mayna, my dear, are you feeling better?" Patricia asked, shooting me a sympathetic look in the mirror.

"...Are you referring to what happened yesterday?" I asked after a pause.

"It's just such a shame! That man—Ray, was it? He really seemed like the honest, faithful sort. He was Prince Dario's bodyguard, so I had the opportunity to speak with him on a few occasions. He struck me as perfectly sensible at the time... Whenever I mentioned you, why, his smile could hardly be contained! Was it really all an act?"

"I don't know. Maybe it was all an act, right from the beginning. Or maybe he meant it at the time, but changed his mind later on." I shrugged my shoulders casually.

At this, Patricia's expression softened with relief. "Oh, I'm ever so glad to see it hasn't hit you too hard."

"Well, I was pretty crushed last night, but then I thought to myself, 'I don't even know him well enough to be heartbroken over him,' you know?"

"Quite right! You'd only known each other a few days, after all."

"Exactly," I nodded. Meanwhile, I ran my fingers through small sections of her fine, delicate hair. Ordinarily these strands were quick to tangle and break, but with my diligent care, her wavy mane became thick, lustrous, and soft. Today, however, her hair felt dry and brittle.

"It feels like the magic has worn off again, Your Highness. I'll renew the spell."

"Oh, yes, please do. The difference is so very obvious whenever your magic wears off... Honestly, I don't know how I could ever live without you, Mayna."

"You're just trying to butter me up," I teased.

Truth be told, it wasn't really a *spell*, per se. Though I was born with the ability, I had never formally learned to use magic. Instead, what I referred to as a "spell" was actually just me focusing my mana into her hair. I did this by running my hands over her waves in sections while silently concentrating on my desire to "make it pretty."

Yes, I know what you're thinking—but believe it or not, this was actually ridiculously effective. Once imbued with my mana, her locks would become smooth and shiny...but only for about three or four days until it wore off, at which point I would need to repeat the process.

"When you do this, does it actually strengthen the hair itself?" Patricia asked.

"No, I'm pretty sure the mana just creates a sort of 'top coat' that sits on top of the strands. That's why it wears off after a few days," I answered as I continued to stroke her hair.

She made eye contact with me through the mirror. "And *all* Flowerfolk are born with mana, right?"

"Well, I haven't done any research on the subject, but I believe so."

Now you may be wondering: What are Flowerfolk?

Flowerfolk are a tribe descended from a union between humans and flower fairies, and as it happens, I am one such individual. Naturally, this means my distant ancestors were flower fairies. That said, we Flowerfolk really don't look any different from ordinary humans. Maybe we tend toward the petite or slender side, but that's about it.

There are some other minor differences, too. For example, we're born with mana in our bodies, while humans are not; we're a bit more sensitive to cold temperatures; we generally like classy or pretty things; the list goes on. Who knows, maybe that last one is part of what drew me to my work as a hairstylist.

"My parents were the only other Flowerfolk I knew of growing up, and we pretty much fully assimilated into human culture here, so... I don't really *feel* like a Flowerfolk, if that makes sense."

"You certainly don't *seem* any different from a regular human...in a good way, of course! Granted, you're the only Flowerfolk I've ever met, but in fiction they're all depicted as vain, fickle, and self-interested. You, on the other hand, are nothing like that."

I smiled sheepishly. "As with actual flowers, I'm sure there are all different types of Flowerfolk out there, too. Maybe I'm just a smaller, more modest blossom."

"You may not be as eye-catching as a rose or sunflower, but I'm sure you're every bit as beautiful."

"Thank you, Your Highness." I appreciated hearing this from her, considering she was so very like a flower fairy herself.

For the record, our world has many other tribes besides Flowerfolk. For example, Dragonkin are one such tribe. Also known as Skyborn, Dragonkin are descended from dragons. There are also Merfolk (descended from mermaids), Treeborn (descended from tree spirits), and Shadowkin (descended from demons). Humans are quite promiscuous...

Of Dragons and Fae

Because Flowerfolk and Merfolk in particular have a long history of mixing with humans, most fairy and mermaid traits have receded, and our innate mana capacity has diminished accordingly. In contrast, Treeborn and Shadowkin have relatively pure bloodlines, and likewise, their mana levels are much higher. Dragonkin, on the other hand, are somewhere in the middle, and they can take both human and dragon form at will.

For the most part, however, humans are the dominant species, followed by Dragonkin, who have an entire nation to themselves. I don't know exactly how large the other four tribes are, but I would wager they're few and far between.

"There we go... Now your hair's nice and sparkly again."

The pale rays of the morning sun made Patricia's waves glitter like the ocean itself. I couldn't look directly at it for too long, lest I find myself entranced.

Patricia looked into the mirror and beamed proudly. "You know, I used to hate having to deal with my wavy hair every day, but thanks to you, now I love it. I'm going to keep you around for a long, long time!"

"Thank you, Your Highness. To be fair, I'm sure anyone could manage the same thing in my place, so long as they have mana and a deep love of hair."

"Yes, well, that 'love of hair' isn't as common as you might think. Most people aren't as single-minded as you are," Patricia said with a laugh.

"Oh, right... Of course."

Frankly, I wasn't sure if that was supposed to be a compliment.

Chapter 3: The Royal Engagement

ONCE I finish styling Her Highness's hair, I'm generally free to enjoy the rest of my day. For the most part, my services are only needed in the mornings and at bedtime, so I typically spend the time in between brainstorming new hairstyles, looking for ornaments to add to my collection, and quietly observing the hairstyles of any nobles who visit the castle to take note of any trends.

That day I was in my quarters, sketching a new hair design, when a servant called upon me and told me that Her Highness was asking for me. Naturally, I headed over to the Princess's royal bedchamber right away.

There, I found her sitting at the table, drinking tea with her three attendants. This little teatime was by no means cheerful, however. Patricia's expression was one of abject misery, and her attendants were struggling to console her.

"Your Highness, it's me, Mayna. You asked for me?"

"Oh, Mayna..." She looked up at me weakly, then heaved a sigh. "It's been decided that I'm to marry the Prince of Vaxwald."

"So it's official, then."

Although the news had not yet been made known to the public at large, it was a secret far too large to be kept, and the castle had long since been buzzing with excitement at the prospect of marriage between our Patricia and Prince Dario of Vaxwald, the kingdom of dragons. Rumor had it Dario's recent visit to Myulan was meant to usher things along in that regard as well.

As a mere hairstylist, I was not privy to the details, but I had seen this coming for a while now. As the younger of two children, Patricia would not inherit the throne here; rather, it was her elder brother who stood first in line. Thus, it made perfect sense that she would be used as a pawn to further the friendly relations between our nation and Vaxwald.

"Are congratulations in order? You seem...in low spirits."

At sixteen and eighteen respectively, Patricia and Dario were quite close in age, and personally, I was inclined to think she could do far worse. Still, perhaps part of her had hoped to marry for love, not political gain. Regardless, as a princess, surely she had been raised to expect this outcome from an early age.

"I mean...he's a *Dragonkin*," Patricia replied, her brows furrowed. "What if he goes on to find his Bondmate after we're wed?"

I hesitated. "Well...I suppose that is a distinct possibility. I'm not sure how it all works, to be honest."

"I did ask him about it, and he promised me that if he does find a Bondmate, he won't give her any special title or preferential treatment. He said it won't be cause for divorce...but even then, who knows what might happen? Why, perhaps he'll ditch me in secret to go see her!"

"Yeah... I'm not sure we can really understand what it means for a Dragonkin to have a Bondmate."

"But it's not just that... I'm scared to marry into a foreign dynasty. Yes, we speak the same language, but their whole country is nothing but Dragonkin, and their culture is different from ours!"

"Indeed it is..." Hoping to inspire a bit of hope in her about the engagement, I continued in a more cheerful tone, "But at the very least, Prince Dario seems like a good man, doesn't he? Gregarious and charming and generous... And just think, someday you'll get to be Queen of Vaxwald! That's something no commoner could ever dream of! What else... Oh, I know! Surely they'll let you bring an entourage along with you, right? Your favorite servants, perhaps?"

"No... I'm not allowed," she replied, pouting her lips. "Once I'm married, all my servants and bodyguards are to be Dragonkin. They don't want a lot of humans in their castle."

"Why wouldn't they let you...?" I muttered under my breath, though a moment later it sank in. Of course they wouldn't allow it. The people of Vaxwald likely wouldn't be receptive to a foreign princess who showed up with an entire entourage.

I snuck a glance at Patricia's attendants. They all hailed from noble families, so chances were low they'd be permitted to leave the country for an indefinite period of time.

"I guess I won't be styling your hair for the wedding, then," I sighed. As disappointed as I was, I had no strong desire to run off to Vaxwald, so I was content to let it go.

But Patricia fixed me with a firm look, like a cat zeroing in on a mouse. "Oh, I'm afraid you're not going anywhere. You're coming with me to Vaxwald," she declared.

I froze. "How?"

"As a profession, hairstyling is no more common there than it is here. And since they have no one fit to replace you, they've granted me special permission to bring you along."

"...What?"

"You'll come with me, won't you, Mayna?"

Seconds prior, my heart was heavy with loneliness thinking we were destined to part ways. Now I wasn't sure how to feel at all. Me? Go to Vaxwald?

Obviously I was honored to be chosen to accompany the Princess. Plus, I didn't mind traveling abroad; I was excited to learn more about other cultures. All in all, it seemed like a rare opportunity best acted upon—an opportunity to hone my craft and acquire new skills.

But for as much as I wanted to agree wholeheartedly, there was one thing holding me back, and his name was Ray Alide.

"Don't get me wrong, I would dearly love to go with you," I began hesitantly, "but as you know, there's someone in Vaxwald I'd really rather avoid—"

"Yes, I know! But you're just going to have to suck it up!" Patricia snapped. "You have to go with me, Mayna! Otherwise I...I won't have anyone else to turn to!" Her anger turned to tearful sobs. "I hardly know anything about Prince Dario, and the whole castle's full of Dragonkin... I don't know who I can trust! I need someone who's on my side. Just one person, so I can feel secure. I *need* you, Mayna, because I know I can trust you!"

I balled my hands into fists. Before me stood a girl of only sixteen, being sent off to a foreign country, away from everything she ever knew, and she was *scared*. Was I really going to reject her on the basis that some guy who dumped me would be there? No. No way. I couldn't possibly abandon her.

With my decision made, I looked into her eyes. "Very well. I'll go with you to Vaxwa—"

"Oh, I just knew you'd see things my way!" Patricia exclaimed with a sunny smile, no trace of tears to be seen. "Thank you, Mayna!"

As she wrapped her arms around me in a big hug, I found myself wondering whether I ought to be proud of the young adult she was becoming...or lament the gullible fool *I* was becoming.

Chapter 4: Into the Dragons' Den

NOW that Princess Patricia was to be wed to the Prince of Vaxwald, arrangements had been made for her to leave the country in just ten days. No sense in dawdling now that the engagement was official, I suppose.

Naturally, this meant that I, too, had just ten days to prepare, and I couldn't afford to waste a moment. First I had to pack, then go and explain everything to my parents, then say goodbye to everyone I'd be leaving behind here in Myulan.

Unlike Patricia, however, I was by no means fated to remain in Vaxwald for the rest of my life. The Princess herself had told me she didn't want to tie me down permanently. "Just until I feel comfortable there," she'd explained. "I imagine it won't take more than a year at most." So that was my plan: to live there for a year and see where it took me.

Near the end of our final days in Myulan, I was summoned to the throne room, where the King and Queen personally beseeched me to look after their little girl.

Then, finally, it was the day of our departure.

On that fine summer day, a massive crowd of commoners and nobles alike (as well as the King, Queen, and Prince) gathered to bid the Princess farewell as she climbed into a splendid horse-drawn carriage. I quietly followed her into it.

From there, the royal cavalcade was organized as follows: two rows of horseback knights at the front to serve as bodyguards, our passenger carriage in the center, and then five more carriages behind us carrying Her Highness's dowry items as well as a handful of servants who would be traveling with us to the border and no further. Lastly, another two rows of horseback knights brought up the rear.

Patricia had been tearful all throughout her final farewells to her parents and for some time afterward, but her sobs finally dried up about an hour into the journey.

"Feeling any better?" I asked as I rubbed her back reassuringly.

"Not at all," she sniffed. "The thought that...I won't be seeing my parents again for who knows how long... Oh, I just can't stop crying..."

"There, there. You're going to have so much fun in Vaxwald, I just know it," I said, hoping to cheer her up a bit. "Aren't you excited to see how all the ladies wear their hair over there? Judging from the knights that came to visit us with Prince Dario, it seems short hair is the standard for Dragonkin men. But what of the women, I wonder? Perhaps they wear their hair long and tie it up, like we do in Myulan. Aren't you curious?"

"No," Patricia replied flatly, glaring at me with puffy red eyes. *Strange... I thought she'd be more enthusiastic. Guess I'll have to use my trump card.*

I held my hands out in front of me, cupping the empty air, and envisioned a bright orange gerbera daisy. Then I focused my mana into my hands—*poof!* A single flower appeared out of thin air, identical to the one I had imagined, and I promptly offered it to the Princess.

"Here. I hope this flower makes you feel better."

Unlike the Dragonkin, whose bodies were built for combat, or the Treeborn and Shadowkin, whose mana capacity made them adept at magic, we Flowerfolk didn't really have any talents...save for this one small special trait.

Unfortunately, one measly flower didn't seem to have much of an impact on her dour mood...so I kept on making daisies in every color until her lap was covered in a rainbow of blossoms. Soon they spilled over to the floor, and by that time, the entire carriage smelled like a garden in spring.

At last, Patricia finally smiled.

"Hee hee... Look at all these flowers! They're so pretty."

"There's more where that came from!"

I kept on producing bloom after bloom until the carriage was carpeted in petals of every hue—at which point my mana finally gave out. *Oh well. At least I managed to make her smile.*

"The pink ones are so cute," Patricia mused as she plucked one from the pile. She brought it to her nose to smell its fragrance, then turned to the window. "How much longer until we reach the border?"

I checked my pocket watch. "Not for a while yet, I'm afraid. At our current pace, it will take five hours to go from the castle to the border... and we've only been traveling for an hour and a half."

And once we made it to the border, it'd take us another six hours to reach the Vaxwald castle proper.

"We'll be stopping to have lunch at some point during the journey, but let me know if you'd like to hop out and stretch your legs before then. It's a sunny day, so be sure to stay hydrated."

It was the end of August, and while Myulan's weather was generally mild, it couldn't hurt to stay cautious. Besides, Patricia's other servants were riding in the carriages behind us, and once we crossed the border, a number of Dragonkin servant girls would be joining us for the second leg of the journey.

"I will, thank you. Goodness, is traveling ever exhausting," Patricia sighed, spinning the daisy between her fingers.

WE arrived at the border just past noon. There, Patricia and I would be parting ways with the Myulan knights and servants; the two of us were to cross the border on foot, along with Patricia's dowry items.

"The Vaxwald convoy is already waiting for us on the other side," I called to Patricia, who was still inside the carriage.

Similar to the Myulan cavalcade, the Vaxwald convoy was flanked by horseback knights on both sides, with a passenger carriage for the Princess in the center. There appeared to be a crowd of Dragonkin onlookers forming in the distance—nearly a hundred people, if I had to guess.

"Looks like you've got quite the turnout, too. It seems the people of Vaxwald have come to welcome you," I told her, my tone encouraging.

"Really?" The tension faded from her expression ever so slightly. As she stepped out of the carriage, the gerbera daisies spilled out with her.

"Well then... Let's be off."

"As you wish, Your Highness."

With a final farewell to the Myulan servants and knights, Patricia slowly crossed over the border. I quietly followed along after her, admiring my own handiwork from behind.

Today I had given her a more refined, polished hairstyle: all of it—bangs included—pulled up into a high fan-shaped bun with a tiara perched in front. It was the sort of look that would go well paired with a wedding dress, and it complemented her large earrings, too. As for myself, I had chosen to keep my hairstyle comparatively plain, with no hair ornaments. I didn't want to distract from Her Highness, after all.

As we approached the Vaxwald convoy, a middle-aged knight near the front of the procession hopped down from his horse and knelt before Patricia.

"From here, we, the knights of Vaxwald, do humbly swear to protect Her Highness Princess Patricia and bring her safely to Prince Dario in the castle. Come this way, if you please." The man rose to his feet and led us to a lovely pale white carriage.

But before Patricia made it inside, the crowd of commoners began to shout:

"ANNUL THE MARRIAGE!"

"What?" Startled, I turned back to look at them. I'd thought they'd turned out in support of Patricia, but on further inspection, the looks on their faces didn't seem very welcoming at all.

"Send that spoiled princess back to Myulan!"

"We don't want some gold-digger spending our tax money on pretty dresses!"

I couldn't believe what they were saying. Spoiled? Gold-digger? Where did this come from? Patricia certainly didn't have this sort of reputation back in Myulan. If anything, she was viewed as the nation's "little royal sweetheart." Granted, she still had a child's sense of self-interest, but she was kind at heart. And while she *was* known to purchase expensive dresses and accessories, she was a *princess*. Surely that much was to be expected.

"What's going on...?" Patricia asked, her eyes wide, her face white as a sheet.

"ANNUL THE MARRIAGE!"

Incensed, the crowd began to close in faster and faster until they were nearly running at her.

"Board the carriage, Your Highness. We'll handle them." The middle-aged knight ushered us inside, then quickly shut the door behind us. "On you go, now!" we heard him tell the coachman, and so the carriage began to move, with knights protecting us on all sides.

But just a few steps later, the procession once again came to a halt as the crowd of protesters moved to block our path.

"Get out of the way, all of you! Doing this will accomplish nothing! The engagement has already been decided!" one of the knights shouted somewhere outside.

"You call yourself a knight?! Don't you care about the future of Vaxwald?!" a protester shouted back. "Surely Prince Dario can find a better queen than *that*!"

"ANNUL! THE! MARRIAGE! ANNUL! THE! MARRIAGE!" the crowd chanted in unison all around us.

At first this protest seemed relatively peaceful, but the argument with the knight had added fuel to the fire, and the carriage shook slightly as someone outside gave it a hard shove.

"I'm scared," Patricia whispered next to me, nearly on the verge of tears. Gritting my teeth, I pulled her into a tight embrace. I could only imagine how the Myulan knights and servants must have felt right now, powerless to do anything but simply watch the spectacle from the other side of the border.

"Don't touch the carriage! Arrest him!" a knight thundered.

Though they may have apprehended the one protester, the crowd quickly devolved into a full-scale riot, and the carriage continued to buck and jolt. Were people inadvertently bumping against the conveyance in the scuffle, or were they actively trying to tip us over?

"Why is this happening?! What did I ever do to them?!" Patricia wailed, shrinking into a tiny ball.

What if these protesters try to board the carriage? I thought in a panic. *What do we do then?*

Surely they'd have the sense to keep their hands off another country's princess, or so I hoped. As for me, however, I was fair game—

Just then, the low roar of a beast shook the carriage. No, not just one—multiple. And I could tell they were coming closer.

"What was *that*?!" Patricia shrieked, clapping her hands over her ears in fright. The cabin of the carriage seemed to vibrate with every growl, and for a moment I wondered if it might shatter the windows.

"Dragons?!" I shouted over the earsplitting roars. "Maybe someone's transformed!"

Was it the knights, or was it the protesters? Regardless, we were in danger. If this was to become an all-out clash of full-sized dragons, our carriage would surely be crushed underfoot.

Then, out of nowhere, the scene fell silent—deathly silent, with no trace of a dragon's beastly cries.

"What happened?" Patricia whispered, and a split second later, the carriage door flew open. I dove in front of the Princess, shielding her.

"Your Highness! Are you all ri—"

Who should walk in but a golden-haired dreamboat—I mean, Ray Alide. The guy who *dumped* me.

You know, it's ironic that a mere knight would look more princely than the actual prince, I snarked internally.

Meanwhile, Ray took one look at me and froze, eyes wide.

"Hi," I greeted him casually.

"What are *you* doing here?" he growled.

"I've come along with Her Highness as her personal hairstylist."

"I personally requested her company," Patricia explained.

Ray glanced at her out of the corner of his eye, then looked back to me and implied, "You didn't decide to...chase after me or anything, did you?"

Mind you, I'm not usually the type to lose my temper, but boy, did that ever set me off. I leapt to my feet.

"*As if!*" Furious at the mere thought, I glared and laid into him, "I don't give a rat's ass about *you*. I came here to *do my job*. Get over yourself!"

"Ray! Is Her Highness safe?" someone called to us from outside the carriage.

At this, Ray snapped back to his senses. He ushered us outside and over to a young man with trim and tidy silver hair. He was shorter than Ray, but more tan and muscular in build.

It was none other than His Highness Prince Dario himself.

"I'm glad you're here, Patricia. What an awful welcome this has been... I'm so sorry."

A handful of protesters were now bound with rope, but they scarcely needed it. Now that Dario was here, the entire crowd was still.

"Your Highness..." Patricia meekly stepped up to him, and as he put a reassuring hand on her shoulder, she continued, "I thought you were waiting for me at the castle."

"Eh, I got bored, so I asked my bodyguards to escort me here...and am I ever glad I did."

"Then...were those roars we heard *your* roars?"

"Yes, I'm afraid so. We came by horse, but when we saw the commotion, we transformed."

Beyond him on the hill, I could see a few horses trotting in our direction to reunite with their masters.

Dario glanced at the crowd, then back at Patricia. "Don't worry. These rioters will be dealt with accordingly. It seems they were only acting out of concern for their country."

"I think they have the wrong idea about me."

"Yes, it seems they've bought into some baseless rumors."

"Where would such rumors even come from?"

"I'm not sure... I'll have my men continue to look into it. For now, I think it's safe to say the true culprit lies elsewhere. Don't worry about it too much, all right? These things happen whenever foreign royalty is introduced to the ruling dynasty. The people worry that an outsider will damage the country, and then they start to take their own paranoia as fact." Dario smiled, flashing his pearly whites. "Just relax. The rumors will die out once the citizens get to know you. They're going to love you, I promise."

For one so young, Dario seemed to have a good head on his shoulders. I could envision the great king he would someday become.

"Okay," Patricia replied, blushing faintly.

"By the way…" Dario began, glancing in my direction, then turned to Ray. "Isn't this the woman you *thought* was your Bondmate? What's she doing here?"

"She's my hairstylist. I got special permission to bring her along," Patricia explained.

"Oh, that's right. I remember you were telling me about her. It seems we meet at last."

Ray scowled as Dario and Patricia continued their conversation. It was my first time seeing him upset, considering he was all smiles back when we were "Bondmates" or whatever.

As Dario grinned mischievously at his faithful bodyguard two years his senior, I remembered how Ray had told me that he both respected His Highness *and* thought of him as a younger brother. Back then, their rapport had seemed rather fraternal indeed—but now Ray seemed to resent every fiber of Dario's being.

"Oh, I know!" Dario exclaimed, clapping his hands together.

"Don't you dare," Ray shot back hastily.

"At least let me finish!"

"That look on your face tells me you're up to no good."

"Nonsense! Perish the thought!" Dario insisted, a playful smile on his lips. "I've decided I'll make you one of Patricia's bodyguards."

"You're demoting me? I thought we had already chosen her guards," Ray countered, quirking a brow.

But Dario didn't miss a beat. "I'm *not* demoting you. This is just a temporary placement," he clarified with a sunny smile. "And while I've already assigned a few men to the task, I'm sure Patricia would feel more secure having someone around that she already knows and trusts. You don't mind joining the team, do you?" He turned to Patricia. "What say you? I'll bet you'd prefer to have at least one familiar face nearby, am I right?"

"Yes, please," Patricia answered dutifully, glancing at me out of the corner of her eye.

I couldn't even begin to imagine how I must've looked in that moment…but I'm willing to bet "Kill me now" was written all over my face.

Chapter 5: Vaxwald Castle

ASIDE from the scuffle at the border, the rest of our journey was fairly uneventful. Occasionally I would spot curious Dragonkin peering at us from the side of the road, but they made no attempt to approach us; either they weren't opposed to the marriage, or perhaps they just weren't brave enough to say so in Prince Dario's presence. Either way, we arrived safely at the Vaxwald castle without delay.

The castle proper was a majestic sight to behold. Built with dull gray slate, it also served as a fortress—quite the stark departure from our charming little white castle back home. One look and I knew I was bound to get lost at some point.

"Nnnn... Everyone in the castle hates my guts, I just know it..." Patricia whimpered. She'd managed to put on a brave face in front of Dario, but evidently it still weighed heavily on her.

"Now, now, don't be silly. I'm sure they're all happy and excited that you're going to be part of the royal family! See?"

As our carriage passed through the castle gates, I pointed outside the window at the crowds, where dozens upon dozens of people were smiling and applauding. Clearly not everyone had bought into the rumors.

The two of us stepped out of the carriage and followed Prince Dario into the castle. Our destination: Patricia's personal quarters.

"Here we are. This will be your sitting room," he explained as we arrived. "It may seem dark now, but that's just because the sun has set. Tomorrow morning, you'll see that it's rather light and airy. Now, if the summer sun gets a bit too hot for you, you can open the door to the balcony to get some air circulation."

In sharp contrast to the austere aesthetic of the castle exterior, the interior design of Patricia's sitting room was downright adorable, with flower-print wallpaper, shag carpet, and brightly colored furniture. When Prince Dario explained that he had customized it to suit her tastes, she looked positively over the moon.

"Next door we have your bedroom; I figure we ought to sleep separately for the next month or so until our wedding night. Oh, and your dressing room is over here, across the hall. Beyond that, we have plenty of other spare rooms, and you're welcome to use them as you see fit."

"Thank you, Your Highness."

"I imagine you must be exhausted from the long journey. I'll have my servants cook you a meal. Then, after you eat, feel free to get some rest. We can introduce you to my parents tomorrow."

The servants got to work at once, preparing food and carrying Patricia's many personal belongings into their proper rooms. One of them tapped me on the shoulder and led me to where I would be staying. Unlike the other servants, who all slept in a dormitory together, I had been assigned a room of my very own, presumably as a courtesy to the Princess. Fortunately, my room wasn't that far from hers, so I didn't have to worry about getting lost in the castle.

"You'll be eating all your meals in the servants' canteen. It's in the North Wing, first floor. We don't have set mealtimes, so you can visit at any time, but be warned that they might not have anything left if you turn up late at night. The bath is right near there, too."

"Thank you."

Having finished her spiel, the servant handed me a candelabra replete with candles, then turned and left. I glanced around the room; it was by no means large, but it was furnished with a loveseat and a writing desk, and the bed was freshly made. All in all, I was grateful.

That said, the closet was (obviously) barren. I needed to go and fetch my—

"This luggage is yours, right?"

A sudden voice behind me nearly made me jump out of my skin. I whirled around to find Ray standing in the doorway, carrying two leather trunks and one large satchel. Behind him in the hallway sat a pile of familiar boxes.

In the dark of the night, his golden hair and eyes were illuminated only by the light of the candelabra.

"How did you know that...?" I asked.

He merely shrugged.

"Well, thank you."

Truth be told, I wasn't exactly comfortable being alone with him in the same room, and yet for some reason he lingered, examining everything from the windows to the carpet to the fireplace.

"What are you doing?"

He didn't answer. But when he started poking around my bed, well, that was where I drew the line.

"Can you leave now?" I asked with a frown.

At this, Ray finally turned and acknowledged my presence. "Do you plan to stay in Vaxwald permanently?"

"No, not permanently. Just until Her Highness has adjusted to her new life here."

"And when will that be, exactly?"

"I couldn't tell you. We were thinking a year or so, but it's really up to her."

"A *year*?"

He scowled. I scowled back. Maybe he wasn't excited at the prospect of spending the next year with me, but I wasn't exactly excited to be around someone who hated my guts, either. Regardless, we both needed to suck it up and do our jobs.

"Just leave, would you?" With a sigh, I turned my face away and reached out to give him a little shove—but before I laid a finger on his armor, he seized me by the wrist.

"No, *you're* going to leave," he growled, taking a step toward me.

Startled by this sudden close proximity, I tried to take a step back, but couldn't wrest myself free of his grip.

"Get out of Vaxwald, Mayna." The candelabra's scarlet flame danced in his eyes. "A year is far too long. Even six months would be too long. No, you're going to leave in one month—just as soon as the wedding ceremony is over."

"Why should—"

"*One month*. Got that?" And with that, he released his grip on my wrist and stormed out of the room.

Once he was gone, I grabbed the first thing I thought of—my satchel—then thought better of it. Instead, I walked to the bed, grabbed a pillow... and flung it full-force at the door.

"*Who died and made you the boss of me*?!"

Chapter 6: The Dragonkin Servants

THE next morning, I was on my way to Patricia's bedroom when I spotted a Dragonkin standing guard outside the door. It wasn't Ray; evidently he had yet to turn up.

Personally, after last night, I was grateful not to have to see him first thing in the morning. *Sorry, Ray, but you don't get to dictate how long I stay here! I'm a grown woman, and I can make my own decisions!*

I walked into Patricia's bedroom to find three Dragonkin servants in the process of washing her face.

"Good morning, Your Highness. Did you sleep well?"

"Oh, good morning, Mayna! Goodness, are you ever a sight for sore eyes. Why, last night I didn't get any sleep at all!"

"Today you'll be meeting with the King and Queen, correct? Perhaps we'd better go with a more subdued style."

"Yes, please! People are already saying I'm some spoiled gold-digger, and I don't want to make it worse!"

As I approached her, one of the Dragonkin servants stepped forward. She seemed to be the leader—tall and aloof, with hard, angular features and long, straight, dark brown hair tied up in a simple ponytail. Not a single strand was out of place.

"You're Mayna, right? Princess Patricia's hairstylist?"

"Yes, that's me," I said with a smile, hoping to soften her unfriendly gaze. Unfortunately, she didn't bat a lash.

"I'm Rebecca. Her Majesty the Queen personally assigned me to look after the Princess, and together with my associates Sari and Mona here, we will be doing just that."

"Sounds great. But her hair—"

"We'll be handling that, too. While none of us are hairstylists by trade, we're all competent enough to get by. Besides, you know nothing of our culture. If the Princess hopes to fit in among the nobility, then she needs guidance from someone who's familiar with Vaxwald dress code."

"Vaxwald *dress code*?" Patricia repeated, looking less than enthusiastic at the prospect.

Rebecca indicated the dress currently hanging on a dress form. "As you can see, our dresses are much the same as Myulan's, except that we don't use petticoats to add unnecessary bulk to the skirt."

Indeed, this Vaxwald dress was much more formfitting by comparison, but it still carried the same air of elegance, laden with frills and lace. Likewise, the servants' uniforms were quite similar to those seen back home.

"Unnecessary? That 'bulk' makes my waist look nice and trim!"

"Be that as it may, at this time of year, all those layers will make you absolutely miserable."

"I suppose you're right... I'm told Vaxwald summers are much hotter than ours. Frankly, I'm surprised how different the weather is between our two countries. We're not even that far apart!"

Evidently Patricia had come around on the petticoat issue—rather quickly, too—so I decided to cut in before the conversation could continue.

"Your hairstyles are rather different as well. In Myulan it's expected for a lady to keep her hair tied up tight in a bun or chignon, but here in Vaxwald I notice it's common to let the hair hang down, either in a simple high ponytail or a half-up style."

In Myulan, a ponytail would be considered the first step to a bun, but in Vaxwald, a ponytail was the *entire* hairstyle. Not only that, but just yesterday I spotted a woman (presumably of nobility) wearing her hair down fully, with only a wide-brimmed hat to cover it. I could scarcely believe it!

"I'm guessing most people in Vaxwald are born with perfectly straight hair, so they don't need to tie it back for it to look neat and tidy. In Myulan, however, a lot of people have thick, unruly curls that look rather undignified when let down. This is why we developed a tradition of wearing it all up. Take your hair, for example; I imagine it would have trouble holding any volume or curl."

My gaze turned to the two other servants standing behind her. According to Rebecca, the girl on her left with the sharp, upturned eyes was named Sari, and the gentle, unassuming girl on the right was Mona.

"Sari and Mona, correct? Sari, I must say, you have the most exquisite platinum blonde hair. I see you're also rocking a ponytail, but with an outward curl at the end there. As for you, Mona, you've chosen an unpretentious half-up style for those chestnut locks. Length is about the same as mine... Oh, but you've got a slight inward curl at the tips. Would any of you mind if I played with it? It just looks so very silky and—"

"Mayna, that's quite enough! Quit fawning over their Dragonkin hair!" Patricia scolded me.

"I'm not *fawning*... You make me sound like some sort of eccentric..."

"When it comes to hair, you *are* an eccentric," she replied flatly, and I got the sense that the three Dragonkin servants were slightly uncomfortable.

"My point is, the three of us will be handling Princess Patricia's hair, and that's final," Rebecca continued, once she'd recovered from the awkward moment. "We have no need of your complicated Myulan hairstyles here in Vaxwald, and as such, your services will not be required. As I understand it, Her Highness only brought you here because she would have felt insecure otherwise, so by all means, have a seat and entertain her. *That* is your job now."

I frowned and looked at Patricia. Her expression was weary, possibly because Rebecca was so intimidating, or perhaps she simply didn't appreciate a servant calling all the shots right from day one. Regardless, she seemed willing to let the Dragonkin have her way...so I decided I would stand behind them and observe their handiwork.

But as Rebecca started to brush out Patricia's hair—

"Ow! Be more gentle!"

"I *was* trying to be gentle... I sincerely apologize, Your Highness." Knitting her shapely brows, Rebecca resumed brushing slower. Evidently Dragonkin women placed just as much importance in their hair as any human would, because she seemed rather nervous to be handling it. Clearly she was well-meaning at heart.

Unfortunately, those good intentions didn't translate to good results.

"That *hurts*! Mayna, take over! She's going to tear my hair out at this rate!"

"I sincerely apologize," Rebecca repeated as she took a step back, brush in hand. Even she knew better than to argue the point any further. She fixed me with a bitter glare...but personally, I was more interested in the brush she was holding.

"That's a boar bristle brush, isn't it? Mind if I touch it?"

"It's just a normal brush. There's nothing wrong with it," she growled, but she relinquished it to me nonetheless. I touched the bristles, and sure enough, I was right. They were unmistakably boar bristles, hard and firm.

"A boar bristle brush is generally the right choice for someone with fine, straight hair, like you. But because Princess Patricia's hair is so thick and curly, a brush with minimal spacing between the bristles, like this one, is liable to get caught in her hair. And because her hair is so delicate, this can cause breakage."

As I spoke, I opened my satchel containing all my hair care tools. Then I reached in and pulled out a few different combs.

"For everyday detangling, you'll want to use a wide-tooth comb, preferably something large and square, like this. I use the wide-tooth comb to get all the big tangles out first, then I follow up with a fine-tooth comb to smooth it out. Now, you'll want to start from the bottom and work your way up, because if you start from the top, the teeth will snag. Here, I'll show you."

"O-Oh... Okay..."

"As a side note, there are many different types of combs—ivory, tortoiseshell, bone, metal, and so on. As a hobby, I like to collect one of each type, but for Her Highness specifically, I prefer to use this wooden one. It's really high-quality, see? Isn't that nice? I bought it from a traveling merchant. He told me it's made from boxwood. Now, boxwood is very delicate and fine-grained, which makes it quite sturdy, or so I'm told. Most wooden combs are quick to splinter, but not this one. It's very easy to use."

"I see..."

"Unfortunately, I only have the one, but I'm happy to loan it to you anytime. You'll want to coat it in flower oil or hair cream just prior to using it. Oil will add shine to the hair, but be careful not to use too much or it'll look greasy. That said, the Princess generally has very dry hair, so you can safely get away with a bit more than usual. Depending on the weather, hairstyle, and how cooperative her hair has decided to be on a given day, you may want to use mousse instead. Mousse is more lightweight than oil, you see. Oh, and another thing. There are a few different kinds of flower oil—"

But right when I was getting into the swing of my explanation, the Princess cut me short once more.

"You're freaking her out, Mayna. Stop talking and finish my hair, would you?"

"Sorry..."

As I meekly resumed brushing Patricia's hair, Rebecca glanced at me out of the corner of her eye. "She's an odd one, isn't she?"

ONCE Patricia's hair was styled, the other servants and I all filed out into the hall.

"Are you sure you want to give out all that technical knowhow for free?" Rebecca asked me.

"Of course," I smiled. "Despite how I may appear, I'm by no means dead-set on working as Princess Patricia's personal hairstylist forever. Once she feels confident that she can live a happy life here, I'll be returning to my home country. Thus, it's only right that I teach you as much as possible before I go. After all, I imagine her thick, unruly hair must seem like a total nightmare to people with flat, straight hair, like yours. Which reminds me...I ended up braiding her hair Myulan-style for today. Is that all right with you?"

All through the braiding process, I had been on edge, expecting Rebecca to jump down my throat at any given moment...but she remained quiet to the very end.

"Yes, of course. It seemed to suit her quite well, after all. In Dragonkin culture, long, straight hair is seen as the ideal, but I get the sense that it would be rather difficult to straighten Her Highness's hair... I'm starting to understand just how much someone's hair type and overall ambience can affect what sorts of hairstyles look good on them."

"Right?" I nodded.

Her expression softened. "The girls and I will do our best to learn as much as we can from you before you leave Vaxwald, but for the time being, *you* should be in charge of Her Highness's hair. Some things are best left to the professionals, after all."

And with that, she turned and strolled off down the hall, Sari and Mona trailing after her. Maybe she wasn't as hardheaded as I thought she was... My heart filled with glee at the thought of the budding friendship between us—

"I always thought she was a bit of a hardass, but it looks like you've gotten through to her."

I nearly jumped out of my skin. I spun around to find none other than Ray standing there.

"Don't scare me like that! I didn't hear you walk over!"

"I wasn't *trying* to scare you. Your hearing is just worse than ours, that's all."

"Did you come here to insult me or what?" I shot him a glare, then decided to head to the servants' canteen for breakfast.

As I was walking away, he called after me, "I overheard part of your conversation just now, and I think it would take too much time to train an amateur from scratch. I'll speak to the palace attendant and have her hire another stylist. That way you can go home that much faster."

I looked back at him over my shoulder. "I'm not leaving until Her Highness feels comfortable on her own."

But Ray didn't back down. "She has His Highness Prince Dario to look after her. She'll be fine."

"Yes, I'm sure she will be...in time," I replied coldly, then turned away and hurried off down the hall.

AFTER my little spat with Ray, I was walking down the covered walkway next to the palace courtyard on my way to the servants' canteen. There, I spotted Mona rushing over to a man I didn't recognize. He had short brown hair and wore a knight's uniform.

"Good morning, Padell! It's lovely to see you first thing in the morning."

This "Padell" gentleman gently embraced her. "Likewise. Nothing brightens up my patrol like getting to see you," he rejoiced. "How much time can you spare?"

"Not much. I need to go get Princess Patricia's breakfast and take it to her."

"Ah, that's a shame. Then again, I'm on the clock myself. What's she like, anyway, this Myulan princess?"

"I've only just met her, but I don't think she's anywhere near as bad as the rumors claim."

They were clearly crazy about each other. As they spoke, they gazed into each other's eyes and smiled as though they were the happiest two people in the world. For someone like me, who was practically married to her job, it was hard to watch without feeling a twinge of envy.

After a moment, the two pulled apart and went back to their work. Mona was headed in my direction, and she quickly spotted me standing there, staring straight at her. She giggled.

"Busted... I promise I'm going back to work now, so please don't tell Rebecca, okay?"

"I won't tell her, I promise. Are you two an item, then?"

"Oh, yes, but we're so much more than that. We're Bondmates!" she sighed, a dreamy smile playing about her lips.

"Bondmates, you say?"

"It's what we Dragonkin call our soulmates. Have you heard of it?"

"Oh, yes, I have. The Princess mentioned she was concerned His Highness Prince Dario might find his own Bondmate someday," I explained, purposefully electing not to mention the "incident" with Ray. "Judging from the way the two of you were interacting, I can only presume true Bondmates share an incredibly flirty...er, *intimate* bond. Even an outside observer like myself can tell just how much you two love each other... I bet you wish you could be with him all the time, don't you?"

Seeing them only served to further drive home the truth that Ray and I were decidedly *not* Bondmates. If we were, then surely he wouldn't be so hostile toward me. At the very least, I couldn't imagine Padell treating Mona like that—not ever.

Mona smiled softly. "Yeah... I admit, I *do* wish we could always be together. But being Bondmates isn't about flirting all the time. The love you have for your Bondmate runs deeper than that, you know? You always want to put their happiness first, no matter what...and as long as they're happy, then your own happiness doesn't matter."

I could see the love shining in her eyes, and paired with the way the morning sun streamed down over her, she seemed to radiate the warmth of a goddess... Personally, I was half-tempted to worship her, just in case.

"Supposing His Highness had a Bondmate... Let's say he hadn't put it together yet, but she had. What do you think she would do? Do you think she would interrupt the wedding between him and his human bride in order to stake her claim?"

"Sure, wouldn't she? Wouldn't you want to be with your Bondmate at any cost?"

"See, I don't think so at all. I think she would keep quiet. After all, interrupting the wedding might cause strife between our two countries, and the Prince would feel just awful about the whole thing. A true Bondmate would never want that for their beloved. They would put the other person first... Wait, why are you praying to me...?" She stared at me as I pressed my palms together in front of my chest.

"You're just such a saint!"

"Hey, c'mon, don't tease me! You're so weird!" She laughed and walked off.

Evidently a Bondmate's devotion was not to be underestimated.

Chapter 7: The Royal Soirée

IT was now my third day in Vaxwald, and a party was to be held at the castle that evening. This was to be Princess Patricia's official debut into Vaxwald society, and all the most influential noble families would be in attendance.

"I'm scared... What if they've all bought into those nasty rumors about me...?" Patricia sighed gloomily as I styled her hair that morning. Present in the room with us were Rebecca, Mona, and Sari.

"Yesterday, when you met His and Her Majesty, what were they like? Were they rude to you?" I asked.

Patricia shook her head. "No, they were both very sweet. Her Majesty the Queen was very interested in my hair."

"I'm glad to hear it! I purposely chose a slightly more intricate hairstyle in the hopes that they might ask how it was done. To break the ice, in other words."

"Oh, it most certainly did! We had the most lovely conversation about hairstyling—warmed me right up! Though I'm not sure what style we should go for today... Do you think I ought to wear my hair in Vaxwald style, like the Dragonkin? But it's such an awful mess when it's let down... It simply won't look nice unless it's done up!"

I watched through the mirror as Patricia pouted and twisted a strand of curly hair around her finger.

"If you'd like to give it a try, then I'm more than happy to help. I'm sure I can make Vaxwald style work for you. But if you really don't want to, then I don't think you have to force yourself. Personally, I believe we look our best when we wear our hair in styles that suit us and make us feel good about ourselves. And just yesterday Rebecca was saying that Myulan style suits you very well."

"She did?" Patricia turned to look at Rebecca, who averted her gaze in mild embarrassment. "Well, since a local thinks so, I'll wear it Myulan-style! Oh, but...what if they think I'm refusing to assimilate into Vaxwald culture...?"

"We'll have you wear a hair accessory that will disprove that very notion."

"How will that work...?"

"You'll see," I smiled. "I'll bring the accessory with me later this evening when I come by to restyle your hair for the party."

THAT night, the royal soirée was held in the Great Hall on the first floor of the castle. The room was illuminated with dozens of lamps and chandeliers, each a veritable spotlight upon the various members of the upper crust all decked out in their finest—so bright you'd scarcely notice it was pitch-black outside. Onstage, a top-class orchestra was playing a gentle melody.

Meanwhile, amid all this decadence, I stood idly near the corner of the room, wearing a dark blue and white gown. My hair was done up in a Gibson tuck, where the ends were quite literally tucked into the rest of the hair, and I had tied a sky-blue satin ribbon over the bun—a nice, summery shade for the occasion.

Her Highness had requested I attend the party "just in case I have the opportunity to introduce you to the Queen or the other noble ladies," ergo, here I stood. And while I appreciated the opportunity to observe everyone's hair firsthand (as well as their reactions to Patricia's hair), I was feeling rather nervous at the thought of being personally introduced by the Princess of Myulan.

The Great Hall was already full of aristocrats, talking and laughing while eagerly awaiting the arrival of the King, Queen, Prince Dario, and his young bride-to-be. It seemed to me like practically *every* Dragonkin woman had a model physique, tall and slender, the majority of whom also had narrow, almond-shaped eyes. In other words, their overall vibe was a lot like Rebecca's. And the hairstyles that flattered them were decidedly *not* big or poofy. They seemed to understand this, because their chosen styles were all straightforward and unpretentious—befitting of long, straight hair like theirs.

"With that perfectly straight hair, they make a simple ponytail look slick and polished... Oh, and that one over there looks great with her hair down... Just one accessory and she's set..."

As much as I wanted to give it a try, I had a feeling it wouldn't look as nice on me. My hair texture was simply too different. Still, I was having a great time people-watching. Nothing quite set my heart aflame like seeing happy people in fancy clothes.

As I was giggling to myself, I suddenly locked eyes with a nearby Dragonkin man—*ugh, it's Ray.*

He started making his way toward me, and I found myself wondering why he bothered talking to me at all, if he supposedly hated my guts so much.

"Do you not think it a tad creepy, standing alone and laughing to yourself?"

"Oh, shut up," I shot back, covering my mouth with my hand. "I was just having fun admiring everyone's hair, that's all."

"Their *hair*? You must be even more of an oddball than I realized during those five days in Myulan."

So he thought I was an "oddball" from the very beginning?

Ray scanned around the room, frowned in confusion, and looked back at me. "What's so fun about it?"

"Don't you see? These women have polished themselves to perfection, just for tonight. They're like jewels—no two are exactly alike. Sure, some of them are still just diamonds in the rough, but with a slightly more flattering hairstyle, I'm sure they'd sparkle like the rest. Look at that young woman in the red dress; I think she'd look better with a more eye-catching style... Ugh, now I really want to go over there and braid her hair...!"

Right as I squeezed my eyes shut and turned away, however, I heard a tiny laugh beside me. Confused, I looked back at Ray to find him gazing at me with a soft, affectionate smile on his face—almost like we'd gone back to those days we spent together in Myulan, you know, before he decided I wasn't his Bondmate.

Naturally, I found this rather alarming. "Why are you looking at me like that?"

"Like what?" he asked, tilting his head slightly. The classy setting seemed to further accentuate his good looks.

"What's with the little smile?"

"What smile?" At this, Ray seemed to snap back to his senses. With a hand over his mouth, he continued, "It's nothing. I was just entertained by your bizarre antics... Anyway, the royal family should be here any moment now." And with that, he hurried off toward the stage.

Bizarre antics? Speak for yourself, buddy!

But before I could begin to process his comment, the orchestra's song came to a close, and the guests burst into applause as the King and Queen made their grand entrance. Then, as Prince Dario and Princess Patricia walked in, the applause grew louder still, much to Her Highness's obvious relief.

Nearby, I could hear some noble ladies talking:

"My, what an adorable little princess!"

"She does seem a bit spoiled, though."

Evidently the room was a mixed bag of those who approved of her, those who had bought into the rumors, and everyone in between. *We'll just have to give it time,* I thought.

"She's human, but I daresay she looks like a Flowerfolk," one of the nobles remarked.

"Indeed, she's quite small and stylish. Fortunate she's human, too, because a real Flowerfolk would *never* do. I mean, you've read *Tales of Tribal Romance*, surely?"

"Oh, yes, I have. I quite liked the one about the Merfolk."

"Likewise. I also enjoyed the one about the human."

I hadn't heard of this *Tales of Tribal Romance* prior to now, but I could only assume it was a Vaxwald thing.

Meanwhile, the nobles' attention shifted to her hairstyle.

"Look at that hair!"

I braced myself.

"It's so lovely!"

Yes!

"Everything about it screams Myulan, but I confess I'm rather curious how they do it."

YES!

Fist-pumping internally, I quietly approached them. I had a goal to achieve, after all.

"Here. This is for you," I said as I took two sheets from my stack of papers and offered one to each of the women, who appeared to be in their thirties.

I had created a step-by-step guide explaining how to achieve Patricia's hairstyle, written in layman's terms, with helpful illustrations for every step. Sketching was a crucial part of my hairstyle design process, and so I was a reasonably competent artist in my own right. This was, of course, done with the full knowledge and consent of His Highness Prince Dario, who kindly made the arrangements to have them copied in bulk in time for the party.

"This pamphlet details Princess Patricia's current hairstyle. It may be too complicated to achieve on your own, but with the help of a servant, it shouldn't be an issue," I explained.

Dubious, the aristocrats took the pamphlets from my hands and stared down at them. "Oh, I see... There aren't that many steps involved..."

Indeed, the process was fairly straightforward. First, I sectioned off a good-sized chunk of hair on each side of her head. Then I took the remaining hair and tied it up in a high ponytail. From there, I twisted the side hair into crown braids, curling up and around the base of the ponytail while incorporating small strands from the ponytail as I went along. Any excess hair was pinned inside the bun to complete the look.

The end result: a crown-shaped bun with a braid wrapped around it.

"This style will look even more lovely when paired with a Dragonkin's naturally straight hair. I hope you'll give it a try; I'm sure it would look great on you."

"I suppose I'll need to teach my servant how to braid, then."

"Your hairstyle is rather fetching, too, if I may say so."

"I have a pamphlet for mine, too, if you like," I replied without missing a beat. "You can easily achieve the same look using a hairband."

I had seen this coming, and so I had mass-copied a how-to guide for my own hairstyle as well. I handed a second pamphlet to each of them; they took it, glanced down at it, then looked back at me.

"Who *are* you, anyway?"

"I'm the Princess's personal hairstylist," I replied with a cheerful smile.

From there, I made my way around the Great Hall, quietly passing out pamphlets to anyone who was interested. Then, before I knew it, the King's royal speech had ended, Patricia had officially been introduced, and the orchestra had started back up again. The nobles began to drink and talk and dance, many of them crowding around the royal family to get a word in.

Meanwhile, Patricia had stepped down from the stage and was now making the rounds from one end of the room to the other. As she approached, the guests began to notice her hair accessory.

"Oh, my, is that a little dragon? And silver, to boot!"

"Not only that, but the eyes are little gray gems... How very clever."

Indeed, her hair accessory was shaped like a dragon, subtly curving along the edge of her bun. It was small in size, but the jewels embedded within were enough to attract plenty of attention.

Patricia was so surprised when I first showed it to her a few hours ago. Truth be told, I'd custom-ordered it from my favorite Myulan craftsman before we left for Vaxwald. I figured Prince Dario would find it flattering, and if I was lucky, maybe he'd come to like her even more as a result. After all, though this was purely a political marriage, it certainly couldn't hurt for the two of them to get along.

Sure enough, His Highness seemed rather pleased indeed. He and Patricia were engaged in a conversation with a noble—perhaps a friend of the family—and Dario was gesturing to the accessory on Patricia's hair, proudly showing it off. The Princess looked pretty happy about this, too.

Perhaps it was too early to tell if the two of them had a romantic interest in each other, but at the very least, they seemed to enjoy each other's company. And with time, perhaps that fondness would kindle true love. It was clear from the way he paid no mind to the rumors that Prince Dario was a level-headed man worthy of our Princess. When I first suggested my pamphlet idea, he laughed and said "It'd be hilarious if this starts a new hairstyle trend!"

All in all, I was starting to see why Ray cared for His Highness as strongly as he did. He was still so young, and yet he felt like a true leader. And in turn, I could see how his popularity with the public would cause them to turn a critical eye on his bride-to-be.

I glanced back at them to find that Dario and Patricia had parted ways while I was distracted. Now Patricia was alone, speaking to a middle-aged man with a large and impressive mustache.

At first the conversation was civil, but then...things went south.

"I've heard a lot of rumors about you lately. They *are* just rumors, I hope? Because I'm honestly not sure. But either way, if you're going to reveal your true colors, I do hope it happens before the wedding ceremony," the man scoffed.

Nearby, Ray was calmly watching the interaction between them. *Is he going to step in if things escalate? And what about Patricia—is she okay?*

I could scarcely stay still. Considering how upset she had been to learn about the rumors in the first place, I worried she might break down sobbing...and yet she merely furrowed her brow.

"Truth be told, I was scared to make my debut at this party. I was concerned that everyone might have bought into those blatantly false rumors about me. But you see, His Highness told me 'anyone so easily duped is not to be trusted in the first place,' so I shan't pay your comment any mind." And with a smile, she walked off.

Meanwhile, I was cheering internally. *That's our Princess!*

Fortunately, this man had the sense not to pursue her. Instead, he was flushed red with rage, fuming at the thought that Patricia had bested him in verbal combat. This time it was *my* turn to speak to him.

"Your Grace?" I called.

He glared down at me. "*What?*" he spat.

"This is for you to take home. If you have a wife or daughter, they might like to have it."

"Yes, I have a wife and daughter. What *are* these?" he demanded, snatching the pamphlets from my hand and staring down at them.

"This one is a how-to guide with instructions on how to create Her Highness's hairstyle. And as a bonus, this one is a guide for my hairstyle as well."

"I don't need this trash! I would never let my wife or daughter wear their hair like that!" He thrust the pamphlets back at me.

"Oh, well, all right. I just thought I'd give it to you, since this style will become a trend soon." I shot a quick glance around the room, where a lot of the noble ladies were reading the pamphlets with interest. "Hopefully your daughter doesn't complain that you didn't bring one home for her. Young people are quick to pick up on new trends, you see."

I turned to leave, but before I could, the mustachioed man snatched the pamphlets back. "I...I suppose I may as well hang onto it," he growled.

"Thank you, Your Grace!" I beamed at him, then walked away.

The next thing I knew, Ray was standing next to me—*wait, wasn't he supposed to be guarding Patricia?* I shot a hasty glance in her direction and spotted other knights standing in her vicinity.

Meanwhile, Ray seized me by the arm and dragged me over to the wall, his expression severe.

"He's a nobody, Mayna. He's not a saint, but he's not a villain. Just leave him be."

I was ready for him to launch into some kind of lecture or tirade, but instead he simply sighed. Then his lips curled in a smirk.

"That said, you got him good."

I smirked back. "I sure did, didn't I?"

Chapter 8: The Hairstylist's Apprentice

PRINCESS Patricia's debut party ended without incident, and the next day, I spotted a handful of women in the castle sporting the same hairstyle, likely having used my pamphlets as a reference. Some of the noble ladies had put their own unique spin on it, too.

"Oh, I'm so flattered that they'd style themselves after me. It feels like they've accepted me!" Patricia gushed as I was putting her hair into bedtime braids that evening.

I had handed out pamphlets of my own hairstyle as well, but naturally a commoner's hairstyle couldn't possibly hold a candle to the Princess's in terms of popularity.

"You're the talk of the town, Your Highness," Mona sighed dreamily. "All the Dragonkin girls are taking note of your hair and fashion sense. Speaking of which, I think I might try a different hairstyle tomorrow... I want to show off for Padell." She was, of course, referring to her Bondmate.

"You do realize he'll swoon over you no matter what your hair looks like, right?" Rebecca teased as she was making Patricia's bed, and Mona grinned sheepishly.

Out of the corner of my eye I noticed that Sari was looking at Mona rather coldly. With her pale, platinum blonde hair and upturned eyes, she always gave off a distant air, but it occurred to me that I had yet to see her smile even once. She spotted me looking at her and turned away, still scowling.

Unlike with Rebecca and Mona, who were starting to warm up to me over time, I still hadn't made a connection with Sari. If I spoke to her, she would rarely even respond, and when she did, she was always detached and formal. In retrospect, this wasn't too terribly different from the way she treated Rebecca and Mona. Perhaps she preferred to keep her work and personal life separate...or maybe she just didn't enjoy her job all that much.

I turned back to the conversation at hand.

"Yes, I imagine you're a star player here in Vaxwald, Your Highness. As a commoner, I couldn't be more envious. I can style my hair however I like and no one would notice, but when it comes to you, why, you can start an entire movement! You're a trendsetter, Princess!"

"In that case, I'd better pay careful attention to my appearance from now on. Especially if I'm going to appear in public."

"Your next big event will be the wedding, I imagine. Now *that* will start some trends—your hairstyle, your dress, everything. All the brides will want to look like you."

Patricia's wedding dress was currently in the process of being tailored, but it was scheduled to be ready in time. As for her hairstyle, I was still in the brainstorming phase. Her dress was going to be pure white, so I needed to come up with something equally pure and innocent, yet still classy and dignified. Something everyone would want to imitate.

THE next morning, before noon, I was visiting Patricia's sitting room to discuss my thoughts about her wedding hairstyle, show her some of my designs, and take note of any requests she had. Partway through, however, there was a knock at the door, and Rebecca went to open it.

"Your Highness, it's Torpan, the palace attendant."

"Let her in."

At the Princess's request, in walked the slender, middle-aged woman in charge of supervising the servants, as well as a young man I didn't recognize, and...Ray? He was supposed to be standing guard just outside. Did he need something from Her Highness? He had a hard frown on his face.

As for Torpan, normally she was so stern in demeanor that she made Rebecca look easygoing by comparison, but in perfect contrast to Ray's dour mood, today she was actually *smiling.*

"Your Highness, I have brought you an apprentice hairstylist who will be taking over after Miss Mayna returns to Myulan."

"You're referring to that gentleman there?"

"Indeed I am. Go on and introduce yourself."

At Torpan's prompting, the young man took a step forward, placed a hand on his chest, and bowed deeply. "I am Kirion Soh."

Kirion looked to be the same age as me, or perhaps slightly younger; a hint of boyishness yet twinkled in his eyes, and he had an outgoing, friendly air about him. He was half a head shorter than Ray, with his long, dark hair tied back in a low ponytail. The average Dragonkin man generally kept his hair short, and yet Kirion's descended well to his posterior. Rarely did I encounter a man with hair as long and healthy as his.

"When I heard that the Princess of Myulan was seeking a hairstylist, I volunteered myself immediately. It would be an honor to work on your hair, Your Highness."

"Kirion here is a barber. He used to work for a merchant and would visit his mansion regularly to work on both his and his wife's hair," Torpan explained.

"Not only can I give haircuts, but I'm also very skilled with my hands," Kirion continued. "While I don't have any prior experience with your intricate Myulan braiding techniques, I've worked with hair for a long time now, so if you're willing to train me, I'm sure I can pick it up in no time flat. Again, it's truly an honor to be here!"

His bright smile was contagious, and Patricia smiled back in kind. "Welcome, Kirion. Mayna here is incredibly good with my hair, and I'd trust her over anyone, but she left her whole family back in Myulan to come here with me, and I don't want to keep her in Vaxwald forever. That's why I'd like for you to train under her and study her methods. Mayna, make a proper stylist out of him before you leave, won't you?"

"Yes, Your Highness," I said with a firm nod. Honestly speaking, I was nowhere near talented enough to take on an apprentice, and as such had never attempted to teach someone before, but I was willing to give it my very best.

But before the conversation could reach its conclusion, Ray cut in. "Wouldn't a female stylist be better suited to the task? Surely one would think it strange to assign a man to handle a woman's hair."

"He's a good worker, Sir Ray. Very diligent and dedicated," Torpan argued. "If you're worried that he'll harbor untoward thoughts regarding the Princess, don't be. He worked on the merchant's wife's hair just fine."

Her sleek ponytail and perfectly pressed uniform gave her a generally uptight vibe, but perhaps she was more lax about opposite-sex interactions than I had given her credit for... Then she placed a protective hand on Kirion's shoulder, and I started to wonder if maybe she was just really fond of him in particular.

"You speak as though you've known him a long time, but you only just met him a few days ago," Ray commented, his suspicion plain.

"Yes, but you see, in all my years I've worked with many a servant, and I can tell at a glance whether they'll be trustworthy."

"Is he?"

"He is. There were a number of other candidates, but I determined him to be the most talented and trustworthy of the lot," Torpan declared proudly.

The two stared each other down in perfect silence. Things were getting nowhere fast, so I decided to take Torpan's side.

"There are male hairstylists back in Myulan, too. The most well-known is the man who personally served the Queen about a hundred or so years ago—he was *so* incredibly talented. He crafted hairstyles in which he would build the hair straight upwards. Sometimes he would style her hair like the ocean and use a miniature ship model as an accessory, and other times he would shape her hair like a birdcage and put live birds inside! All done with the power of braids, of course! He went down in history as the original inventor of *many* strange and unique hairstyles."

"Goodness, it sounds as though male stylists have been around for at least a *century*! Nothing strange about it then, is there?" Torpan fixed Ray with a smug smirk.

Kirion turned to me. "You sure know your stuff, Miss Mayna!"

But when I looked into his dark eyes, I felt...*restless*. Not the flutter of budding attraction—no, this was something else. Something I couldn't quite place...

"Mayna!"

At last, I managed to tear my gaze away from Kirion's. I turned to find Ray glaring daggers at me. Perhaps he was angry that I had taken Torpan's side in the debate...

IN the end, Ray was so completely opposed to Kirion taking the job that he went straight to Prince Dario about it. His protests were ultimately in vain, however; the Prince was not the type to judge a book by its cover, and he was content to let Kirion stay as long as he proved he was the right person for the job.

And so Kirion Soh was officially appointed as my apprentice.

"I'm excited to be working with you, Miss Mayna!"

"Likewise, Kirion, I look forward to teaching you."

For lack of a better place to go, I led him to my quarters so we could show each other the tools we were most accustomed to using. As it turned out, Kirion had far more of a collection than I did when it came to male-targeted hair care items. I'd worked on men in the past, and so I stocked the bare minimum necessary for trimming and shaving, but his sheer variety of gels, shaving creams, and razors had me all agog.

"What beautiful hairdressing scissors! They're not bulky, either—I already feel right at home using them!"

"They're nice and sharp, too. I see you've got a whole selection of brushes and hair oil and pins here...not to mention all these decorative accessories! You could open your own shop with all this!" Kirion exclaimed as he opened a wooden box full of hair accessories. Although I made sure to dispose of any that grew rusty or otherwise fell out of fashion, I still had three whole boxes' worth.

As we were fawning and gushing, I caught sight of Ray standing in the corner of the room.

He had tagged along right from the moment I invited Kirion back to my quarters, standing behind me and exuding a venomous aura. I wasn't sure why he had bothered to come with us, but his presence was clearly making Kirion uncomfortable, and frankly, it was a buzzkill.

"If you came here just to glare at Kirion, then please leave," I sighed. When he didn't budge, I pushed the point, "I really don't know what you expected. *You're* the one who asked Torpan to hire a new hairstylist. I get that you don't like him, but everyone else does. You should try not to be so openly antagonistic towards people you don't like, because believe it or not, it really hurts."

Trust me, I would know.

As I pushed him toward the door, his expression grew conflicted, like he was tempted to say something...but whatever it was, the words never came. In the end, he trudged from the room of his own will.

Once I had shut the door behind him, I turned back to Kirion. "Sorry about that. He's just really protective of His Highness Prince Dario—he cares for him like a younger brother. So when it comes to the Prince's bride-to-be, he can't help but want to protect her, too. It's nothing personal."

Kirion gazed at the now-shut door through which Ray had disappeared. "I can't deny that might be the case, but to me, it seems a lot more like *you're* the one he's trying to protect. Are you two an item?"

"Wh—No! Don't be silly!" I snapped hastily.

His lips curled into a playful smile. "Oho? Something's definitely going on here. Is he your ex or something?"

"Nngh..." I couldn't exactly deny it.

Kirion's smile broadened. "Oooh, I *love* boyfriend-girlfriend drama!"

"Really? I didn't peg you for the type."

"Okay, so he's totally your ex, right? And he wants you back?"

"He does *not* want me," I corrected him.

Instead of letting him jump to conclusions about the situation, I decided to give him the gist of what had happened between myself and Ray—that he had mistaken me for his Bondmate, then ultimately changed his mind before we ever got together.

"Is it even possible to make a mistake like that?"

"I admit I asked myself the same question, but if it wasn't possible, then it wouldn't have happened. Anyway, wouldn't you know better than

I would? You're the Dragonkin here."

"I guess so..." Kirion muttered vaguely. Then he suddenly brightened up. "Well then, if you're not with Sir Ray, then that means I could have a chance with you, right?"

His tone was lighthearted, so I laughed. "Trust me, I'm done with romance after that."

But Kirion kept going. "Aww, c'mon. Just because it didn't work out your first time?"

He was a walking contradiction—the innocence of a boy paired with the charm of a full-grown man. He looked down at me, and as I gazed back into his eyes, once again I found myself oddly restless. I wanted to look away, but somehow I couldn't.

Then I saw my own entranced expression reflected in his eyes, and I snapped back to my senses. Turning my face away from him, I hastily gathered up the accessories lying around and returned them to their proper container.

"My job is more important to me than having a relationship."

Kirion chuckled and shrugged. "I guess you're just that dedicated."

AFTER three days of working with Kirion, I found him to be a good and honest person—smart and talented to boot. He was a quick learner, and whenever my explanation fell short, he was quick to fill in the gaps using his own intuition.

But if there was one observation I could make, it was that he was rather chatty. He would gossip with Mona about the latest scandals in the aristocracy, and sometimes he would fill me in on the secret factions he'd discovered amongst the servants. Either he came across this information incidentally while chatting up a storm with half the castle, or he was intentionally seeking it out to slake his thirst for drama.

Lately he had started to enjoy the negative attention from Ray, too. Evidently he had quite the thick skin. At first I felt sorry for him and thought about telling Ray to back off, but then I noticed that Kirion seemed a bit too eager to provoke him—leaning in close to me whenever he knew Ray was watching—and at that point, I abandoned any notion of choosing sides.

If anything, I couldn't comprehend how Ray could get angry at the mere sight of Kirion within close proximity to me. It didn't make sense. What was he thinking?

As the days passed, Princess Patricia grew more and more at home in Vaxwald. I could wager a guess that the kind gestures from the royal family had helped a great deal—not just from Prince Dario, but from Her Majesty the Queen as well.

"Her Majesty invited me to tea tomorrow afternoon! She told me she can't wait to see my next hairstyle. She also mentioned she'd like to see me try something more Vaxwaldian... Something that isn't a bun..."

While the Princess seemed excited at the prospect of attending a royal tea party, she couldn't quite hide her unease.

"Well then, tomorrow we'll just have to try the Vaxwald style," I nodded.

"But I just know it won't look nice on me! My hair's too poofy!"

"I could use hair gel to contain it, but that might give it an odd sheen... Plus, it would make the hair unnaturally firm, to the point that it won't rustle in the breeze... Hmm. I'll have to come up with a solution that doesn't use gel," I concluded.

Behind me, I could feel Kirion's eyes on me.

Chapter 9: A Minor Incident

ON the day of the tea party, I went in the afternoon to style Patricia's hair. I had already braided it once that very morning, of course, but I wanted to start fresh.

"So, how many guests are coming to this party?" I asked as I brushed out her hair.

"Oh, not that many. Just the Queen, her three attendants, and me."

I nodded. "Let's see, then... Your hair will have a bit too much volume if we let it all down at once, so let's go with a half-up style."

In accordance with Vaxwald style, I left the upper half in a simple ponytail...but Patricia looked into the mirror and frowned.

"We can't leave it at this! Why, it looks as though I just rolled out of bed! Besides, the tea party is going to take place out in the garden, or so I'm told. It'll get all messy at the slightest breeze!"

"Don't worry. I'm going to curl it next."

As I spoke, I took out one of my metal hair irons. I had three different kinds in my possession: straightening irons to straighten the hair, crimping irons to create deep waves, and curling irons for curls and ringlets. On this occasion I was going to need the curling iron, and for that purpose I had already loaded up the fireplace with three logs' worth of kindling. It was by no means a roaring fire, but in the summertime, even the smallest flame was sweltering.

This technique involved placing the metal iron directly into the fire—but only for a very specific amount of time. Let it overheat and the iron would burn the hair, causing serious damage. Thus, in the event the iron was left in for too long, I would need to apply a damp cloth to the metal in order to cool it down.

These curling irons went cold rather quickly, and they needed to be reheated multiple times in order to finish a full head of hair. As luck would have it, I had two at my disposal, which meant I could have Kirion at the fireplace heating one while I was curling Patricia's hair with the other. However, because these tools were somewhere in the neighborhood of two hundred degrees when fully heated, I needed to take extra precaution not to touch her ears, neck, or other bare skin, lest I give her a contact burn.

Fortunately, because Rebecca and the other servants were there to fan her, Patricia herself wasn't suffering too badly from the heat, but I was a different story. Sweating mildly, I worked to curl the lower half of the hair, as well as the ponytail itself, into large, prominent ringlets. At the end, I applied a small amount of mousse for hold, then imbued the hair with my mana to give it extra shine. With this, her style would have staying power without any unnatural stiffness—and the result was quite classy.

Not that Patricia's natural loose curls weren't adorable in their own right, but for this look, I needed to wind the hair tightly so it wouldn't lose its shape. Thankfully, one benefit to naturally curly hair was that, obviously, it was already good at holding curls.

Admittedly, perhaps it would've been more in line with Vaxwald style to straighten her hair instead, but with her natural hair texture, it simply wasn't going to look as sleek and flat as a Dragonkin's, and the end result would no doubt be disappointing. All told, our Princess simply looked better with curls.

"Oh, it's *beautiful*, Mayna! It's ever so fanciful and grand... Why, believe it or not, I actually feel like a princess!" Patricia exclaimed, turning her head every which way to admire her hair in the mirror, her ringlets bouncing with every movement. Personally, I was glad she liked it.

"She really does look the part," Rebecca mused.

"I just love this style of curls! I want to try it someday!" Mona gushed. Meanwhile, Sari eyed Patricia enviously.

"Now for the finishing touch, we'll just add a hair accessory, and then we're all done," I explained, but when I looked over at the table, my accessory boxes were nowhere to be found. I turned to Kirion. "Where did you put the accessories?"

Yesterday he had offered to polish them for me as part of his trainee duties, and I was hardly going to say no. But I only handed them over on the condition he brought them back before the tea party.

"Kirion?"

I looked over to find him staring at the floor, shifting around slightly. Come to think of it, he'd been acting a little strange all morning.

"What's wrong? Was there a problem? You know you can come to me with—"

"I'm so sorry, Miss Mayna!" Kirion cut in loudly, squeezing his eyes shut.

Patricia and I stared at him in wide-eyed surprise.

"The truth is, when I woke up this morning...the boxes weren't on the table where I left them!"

"Well, they didn't just evaporate into *thin air*," Rebecca snapped. "Surely you must know where they went."

"If I did, we wouldn't be having this conversation!"

"Are you trying to suggest someone else moved them?"

"...Last night, after I came back from my bath, I realized I'd accidentally left my chamber door unlocked. Someone must have gone in there and taken them while I was away, I'm sure of it! Although...I went straight to bed that night, so I didn't notice the boxes were gone until this morning..."

Kirion shrank back under pressure from Rebecca. I put a hand on his shoulder.

"I wish you would've told me this as soon as you noticed it... Honestly, who could have possibly taken them...?"

"Good grief, Kirion! My things are in there, you know!" Patricia pouted. Indeed, while two of the boxes contained my own personal collection, the third was reserved for Her Highness.

Personally, I was less than enthused at the prospect that someone had stolen them. I was very fond of those accessories, some of which were one of a kind—but more importantly, if I had inadvertently cost the Princess her entire highly valuable hair ornament collection, I was in deep trouble.

"I'm so terribly sorry, Your Highness," I apologized, bowing my head.

"Just find whoever did this and get them back, all right? We can't have a thief milling about the castle. Go and get in touch with Prince Dario, the palace attendant, and whoever else you need to."

"Right away, Your Highness. I promise I'll find them." I bowed my head once more.

The Princess was generally forgiving of these sorts of mistakes—she'd pout for a bit, but she wouldn't get angry. On the contrary, she would often keep a level head and come up with a solution to the issue, just as she was doing now. It was for this reason that I held a deep respect for her.

"Now what are we going to do? I can't very well attend the Queen's royal tea party without wearing an accessory," Patricia continued with a frown. "At first I assumed the thief was only looking to take my valuables, but now that I think of it, is it possible they were looking to embarrass me in some way?"

"...I can't say for sure what their motive could have been, but rest assured, you'll be just fine. We have plenty of things we can substitute in place of a proper hair ornament." As I spoke, I gestured for the servants to open Patricia's jewelry box. "For example, we could use this pearl necklace, or this piece with evenly spaced gems... All we'd have to do is place it along the hair, like so."

"Oh my, how lovely," Patricia exclaimed.

"You look like an angel! Or a fairy!" Mona squealed.

This look, however, was not my proposed solution for today. I removed the necklace from her hair. "We can use brooches, too...but with this style, I'm thinking we should use fresh flowers."

"But it's already late summer. The selection will be limited," Rebecca pointed out. She, of course, didn't realize who I was or what I was capable of.

Grinning, I magically produced a series of tiny flowers, trimmed away the leaves, stalks, and pollen, and placed them in the Princess's hair—shades of pastel pink, yellow, aqua blue, and white. If this was an evening affair I might've gone with one large bloom instead for a more subtle look, but since this was a garden party, I wanted to go with something bright and festive.

"Are you a mage?!"

"No, I'm just a Flowerfolk. Making flowers is our one specialty."

"You're a *Flowerfolk*? I had no idea!"

The three servants stared at me in surprise. Patricia, of course, wasn't surprised in the least; she was enjoying the floral fragrance with her eyes closed.

"The best thing about fresh flowers is the scent, wouldn't you say?"

And with that pressing concern dealt with, it was time to solve the mystery of the missing ornaments.

Chapter 10: A Request from the Queen

FIRST, we went straight to Torpan to ask for her help in tracking down the culprit. As it turned out, she was more than happy to drop whatever she was doing in order to help us (and by "us," I mean Kirion).

Strangely enough, however, we managed to find the missing hair ornaments the very next day. According to Ray, he had discovered them sitting on the ground outside the castle, tucked away in a quiet spot generally devoid of foot traffic. And miraculously enough, the entire collection was completely intact, all three boxes' worth.

"Thank you so much, Ray!" I exclaimed, beaming at him. Honestly speaking, I had half a mind to hug him—but obviously that wouldn't go over well, so I refrained.

"'Twas nothing, my lady," Ray replied playfully, genuflecting before me in true knightly fashion. Together in the room with us were Patricia's three servants as well as Kirion, who looked incredibly relieved to hear that the stolen items had been recovered.

"I'm amazed you managed to find them out there," I continued. "How'd you do it? Surely there's no way it could have been a coincidence." After all, it wasn't the sort of place you'd visit unless you had a good reason to do so.

But Ray didn't respond. Instead, he turned away as if he hadn't heard a word I said. *Uh, hello? I'm talking to you!*

"Maybe it was your scent?" Mona suggested. "See, I was wondering why you always smelled like flowers, but once you told us you're a Flowerfolk, it all made sense!"

"Wait, what? I smell like flowers?"

"Yeah! I mean, to be fair, we Dragonkin have a really sharp sense of smell—probably sharper than either humans *or* Flowerfolk—so it's possible we're just quick to pick up on other people's body odor..."

At the phrase "body odor," I shifted uncomfortably. Granted, in terms of odors, I could do a lot worse than flowers, but still... Hoping no one was paying attention, I covertly brought my nose within range of my armpit. *Note to self: check frequently to ensure I don't stink.*

"Regardless of our innate olfactory abilities, I couldn't possibly have caught a tiny trace of her scent, you know, obviously. I'm not a *dog*," Ray shot back flatly.

"Right. *Obviously*," Mona snorted. Her choice of emphasis seemed to have further implications to which I was not privy.

Regardless, I wasn't going to press the issue. I concluded that Ray must've simply found them by chance, or perhaps one of his subordinates found them while on patrol and tipped him off. Once we took the matter to Torpan, she'd instructed all the servants in the castle to aid in the search, so maybe the culprit got cold feet about the theft and chose instead to dispose of the evidence in a secluded location. For this reason, I was pretty sure embarrassing Patricia was *not* their motive. After all, if that was their goal, surely there were countless other more effective ways to go about it.

That said, with no way to find the culprit, we would never learn the truth, and so we had no choice but to stay on guard in case an enemy of the Princess was lurking somewhere in the castle.

"I'm just glad we managed to find them," Rebecca remarked.

"Sorry for all the trouble," I apologized with a weary smile.

"You must be *exhausted*. You've been searching nonstop since yesterday! Why don't you get some rest?" she suggested.

"Yeah!" Mona chimed in. "And eat a good, hearty meal while you're at it. You eat like a bird!"

"I do?"

The three of us often took our lunch breaks together; at some point they must've overheard me asking the canteen worker for smaller portions. That said, my requests were by no means drastic—two pieces of meat here, half a bowl of soup there—so I didn't consider myself a particularly light eater. If anything, Dragonkin had oversized appetites!

But nevertheless, Rebecca and Mona seemed quite worried for my health.

"What is it? Do I look pale or something...?"

"No, not at all. It's just... You mentioned you're a Flowerfolk, so I can't help but be a little concerned," Rebecca explained. "I mean, we Dragonkin tend to view Flowerfolk as small and fragile—like a flower, you know? But maybe that's just because we're more on the brawny side."

"Yes, they say Dragonkin are a hardy tribe," I replied. "Now that I think about it, perhaps Dragonkin and Flowerfolk are on opposite ends of the spectrum, with humans, Merfolk, Shadowkin, and Treeborn somewhere in the middle. Though I don't think we Flowerfolk are quite as frail as you imagine us to be. In my opinion, we're really no different from humans."

"You sure about that?" Rebecca asked dubiously.

I laughed. "Don't worry. I've never once thought of myself as weak or delicate. I'm not even that tired right now. I do appreciate your concern, though."

Meanwhile, Kirion and Sari were having a cheerful conversation as they admired the recovered hair ornaments. Naturally, Kirion was his usual friendly self, but personally I was surprised to see that Sari was actually smiling for a change. *To think someone can actually melt her icy façade... Wait. Am I seeing things, or is she blushing?*

Upon further contemplation, it occurred to me that Torpan was quite smitten with Kirion, too. Perhaps he had some sort of natural talent for charming the aloof, uppity type... Maybe he was a con artist in his past life.

A few hours after the accessories were found, I received a special request from the Princess: "My ringlets were a hit at the tea party—and Her Majesty said she wants you to style her hair, too! Could you come with me to her chambers tomorrow morning? Oh, and she wants you to do the same for her three attendants, too."

"Of course, Your Highness. It would be my honor," I answered promptly.

And so, the next day, the two of us plus Kirion set off for the Queen's royal chambers.

Of Dragons and Fae

WHEN we arrived, sure enough, four women were waiting in the room. The Queen looked to be in her forties, with her three attendants all perhaps slightly younger; I was told they hailed from aristocratic families, and indeed, they looked every bit as proud and haughty as one would expect.

"So you're the hairstylist. I've been expecting you."

"Greetings, Your Majesty. My name is Mayna Spring, and this is my apprentice, Kirion Soh."

"Well then, Mayna, I should like you to style my hair at once. I have grown so terribly bored of my current style, you see."

The Queen was a beautiful woman with pale lavender hair and a frank personality. Like most other Dragonkin, she was tall and slender, but the Queen in particular was endowed with a hefty bustline. And as with her three attendants, her hair was long and perfectly straight, presently cascading over her right shoulder.

"We want to have ringlets like the ones you gave Patricia yesterday."

"In that case, I'll need to use my curling irons. Not only can it create curls, but it can produce elegant waves as well. That said, with straight hair like yours, I can't guarantee that it will last for very long. The hair simply isn't predisposed to holding curls, Your Majesty."

"Oh, that's all right. If it lasts long enough that I can surprise the King for lunch, then that's good enough for me," the Queen answered with a mischievous giggle.

And so Kirion and I kindled a small fire in the fireplace and set about heating the irons. Then, once each of the four had determined her desired hairstyle, I immediately got to work.

Even with the balcony door open and a kind servant fanning me, the room was still sweltering—and I would need to do three more heads of hair after this. I hadn't anticipated that all of them would want a wavy style, so this was a lot more work than I initially expected...but still, I didn't want to betray their high expectations. If I was going to do this, then I wanted to do it perfectly.

"Are you okay? Should I take over?" Kirion offered quietly. As much as I appreciated the thought, I knew he had no prior experience with curling irons, and I couldn't very well subject the Queen or her attendants to an amateur. Not only was there a risk of contact burns if the metal touched her skin, but excessive exposure to the intense heat could burn her hair, and then we'd *really* be in trouble. A woman's hair was tantamount to her femininity itself, and as such, it was invaluable.

"Thanks, but I'll be fine," I replied, sweat beading on my brow.

Meanwhile, Patricia and the Queen were engaged in conversation:

"How are things with Dario? Are you getting along?"

"Oh, we most certainly are, Your Majesty. I understand he was rather busy yesterday, but nevertheless, he still set aside time to come and visit me in my chambers. He clearly cares for me. He wanted to know if I was adjusting to life in Vaxwald."

"It must be quite the culture shock, living in a different country in which you are the minority."

"I admit I was nervous at first, but I've since come around. There are so many kind people here...especially you, Your Majesty!"

"Oh, I'm just happy to dote on my new daughter, that's all."

I smiled to myself as I listened to their sweet little exchange. I was so glad to know that the Queen had accepted Patricia in spite of the nasty rumors about her floating around the kingdom. In my opinion, she and her son Dario were both crucial pillars of support in this trying time.

Once I finally finished curling all four heads of hair, the next step was to style it. Then, at long last, my work was finished.

"It's so very elegant and beautiful," the Queen remarked. I had tied her hair loosely at the base of her neck so as to keep those soft, flowing waves in line. Then I took her long, newly wavy bangs and pinned them back to cover her ears. With the ears covered, it produced an elegant and seductive look; conversely, exposing the ears would create an energetic, youthful effect.

The three attendants were all quite satisfied with their styles, too:

"Look at me! I'm like a whole different person! Why, I can't wait to go home and show my husband!"

"I bet he'll flip!"

These women were all twice my age and long since married, and yet they were squealing with delight as if they were young maidens all over again. The sight warmed my heart. Moments like these made my job worth doing.

"Thank you, Mayna," said the Queen, her lips curled in a contented smile as she handed me my pay. It was a lot more than the work itself warranted, but I figured it'd be rude to decline payment from the royal family, so I graciously accepted.

After that, Kirion and I packed up our styling tools and left Patricia to enjoy a pleasant conversation with the Queen and her attendants.

"We can split this between us later," I said, holding up the small sack of reward money as we walked through the corridor.

"Oh, no, that's okay. I barely did anything at all. You should keep it."

"No, that wouldn't be right. You helped, and you deserve your fair share," I insisted.

"You're a real goody-goody, aren't you?" he replied, smiling faintly. "You work hard, you have ambition, and yet you still manage to put other people first. I'll bet you've put in a ridiculous amount of effort to hone your skills, too. You have a purpose in life, and so you have no reason to covet the achievements of others."

"...Where did that come from?"

Ostensibly he was paying me a compliment, and yet his flat, detached tone made me feel more like a research specimen.

But then he grinned.

"I was just thinking you're probably not that popular with the gents," he teased. "You've got a pretty face, but I wager you don't get approached too often—because you don't let yourself *appear* approachable."

"Mind your own business, okay?" I was starting to have second thoughts about splitting the reward with him.

"Personally, I find so-called 'untouchable' women like you *far* more interesting. Makes me curious to see what you'd be like if you actually fell in love."

At this, I looked away. His gaze was starting to make me feel restless again, to the point I was concerned he could hear my heart pounding.

Just then—

"Kirion!"

At the end of the hall stood Sari, her hand raised in a shy wave, to which Kirion waved in return.

"I'm almost done here," he called back. "I'll just be a minute."

My personal quarters were just a few steps away, so the two of us promptly carried the hairstyling equipment inside.

"I see you've made friends with Sari, too. That's something I haven't managed yet, so if there's some kind of trick to it, I'm all ears."

"There *is* a trick...but it's a secret. Likewise, if there's a trick to getting to know *you* better, by all means, let me know." With a wink, he turned and walked out, leaving me rooted to the spot.

Why would he care about getting closer to me when he clearly already had Sari wrapped around his little finger? Or did he simply want to be *good friends* with both of us? Either way, Sari was obviously interested in more than friendship.

Good grief, what a little con artist he is. I plopped myself down on the loveseat and heaved a sigh.

"I'm beat..."

I'd had this funny feeling in my chest for a while now. Wiping my sweaty brow with a handkerchief, I leaned my full weight against the backrest. The castle was already humid from the summer weather, but on top of that I'd done four heads' worth of curling work, too. Maybe the heat was getting to me. I had a headache, and my fingers felt tingly for some reason.

Now that I was finally off my feet, it was hard to motivate myself to get up again, but I needed a drink of water. I pushed myself to my feet, left my room, and headed for the servants' canteen on the first floor.

Ugh, I'm getting dizzy... Clutching the handrail, I guided myself down the stairs. But just as I arrived at the covered walkway that lined the inner courtyard, I exhaled and came to a stop. My head was spinning, and I was starting to think I might not make it to the canteen in time to stop myself from passing out altogether. Instead, I decided to sit down on a nearby bench and catch my breath.

There were a handful of benches here in the courtyard, but the one I chose was nice and shady. Sitting down wasn't much of an improvement, so I lay down on my side instead. The wood was cool to the touch. Perhaps it was well-shaded at all hours of the day.

I'll just rest up here for a bit and then I'll go get some water, I thought as I closed my eyes.

What I didn't realize until that moment, however, was that over in this particular corner of the courtyard, my bench was positioned in such a way that no one could see me lying here—

"I knew I'd find you here!"

In the distance, I heard Mona's voice. I opened my eyes. Had she been looking for me?

This soon proved not to be the case. In the far distance, I could make out two figures—Mona and her Bondmate, Padell.

"Yeah, I could tell you were nearby," he replied cheerfully.

As with the previous tryst I had inadvertently witnessed, the two of them shared a brief embrace, then went back to their respective tasks. Normally I enjoyed watching other people be happy together, but right now I felt like crying. *What if I die alone here and no one ever finds me?*

Admittedly, I was being needlessly dramatic over a little heat exhaustion, but still.

Just then, someone dashed down the walkway and into the courtyard, gasping for air. It was Ray. He glanced around the area, then inexplicably turned and made a beeline directly to my bench.

"Mayna!" He rushed over to me, his eyes wide in shock.

"Ray? What's wrong...?" I asked weakly, struggling to keep my eyes open.

He put his hand to my forehead, gauging my temperature. "When I went to the Queen's chambers to take over guard duty for the Princess, I noticed the room was like a furnace. Then they told me you'd been curling hair for hours in there. I had a feeling it might've given you heatstroke, so I thought I'd check, and sure enough."

So you noticed the room was hot...and your mind went straight to heatstroke? I thought vaguely to myself. He was clearly alarmed—proof enough that he was genuinely concerned for my well-being. But why? Not like I died or something.

"How did you know I was over here?"

But instead of responding to my question, Ray straightened up and walked off. *Are you just going to leave me here?* I wondered. This, too, proved not to be the case, as he soon returned, a drinking glass in one hand and a pail of water in the other. He sat the pail down next to my bench, then pulled me up into a sitting position and handed me the glass of water.

"Thank you."

"Yeah, yeah. Just drink it, will you?"

As he propped me upright, I took small sips from the glass.

"Need more?"

"No, this is enough," I answered faintly, closing my eyes.

He laid me back down onto the bench, then pulled a hand towel out of the pail of water, wrung it out, and laid it onto my forehead. *Ahh, nice and refreshing.*

Then he pulled out a second towel, wrung it out, and wrapped it around my neck. Perhaps my neck was more sensitive to the cold compared to my forehead, because the excess heat seemed to vanish instantly. Maybe the towels were absorbing it; they soon grew warm, and Ray had to re-dampen them with some frequency.

For a while I simply lay there in silence and let Ray take care of me, but as my condition improved, I found the strength to open my eyes once more.

"How are you feeling?" Ray asked, clutching my sweaty hand in his. His skin was damp and chilly to the touch.

"I think I'm feeling better now. Thank you."

"We should have a doctor examine you, just in case... Let's get you to the castle infirmary. I'll carry you there."

"You don't have to—" My weak protests fell on deaf ears.

\

He scooped me up into his arms, bridal style, and carried me all the way to the infirmary. Between his natural good looks and his prestigious position as Prince Dario's personal bodyguard, Ray attracted attention like a magnet everywhere he went, and I could feel everyone staring at us as we passed. *Ugh, how humiliating.*

"Doc, you in?" Ray called as he opened the infirmary door and carried me inside. Sure enough, there stood a gentleman in a white coat—forty-something, unshaven, his clothes messy and wrinkled—presumably the doctor.

"Well, if it isn't our very own Sir Ray Alide! What happened to your lady friend there?"

"She has heatstroke. Please examine her."

"Heatstroke? Strange... She must be quite sickly for a Dragonkin."

"She's a Flowerfolk, actually. Now please examine her—I'll put her down on this cot."

"Wh—You can't just—Well, all right. Have you given her any water?"

"Yes, sir."

Once Ray had laid me down onto the medical bed, the doctor came over, removed the towels, and felt my skin directly.

"Please don't touch her too much."

"Do you want me to examine her or not, boy?" the doctor snapped back. "At any rate, she's going to be fine, thanks to your excellent first aid. This *was* your doing, right?" he asked, holding up the hand towels. "Come to think of it, you came and asked me about heatstroke just the other day, didn't you?"

He did? I turned and looked at Ray.

"Even on the hottest summer days, Dragonkin scarcely ever get heatstroke, so I admit I was confused why you'd want to know. Now it all makes sense. You were concerned for this Flowerfolk," the doctor concluded.

"You don't mind if she rests here for a while, right?" Ray asked in a hard voice that suggested he wouldn't take no for an answer. Evidently he was in no mood to respond to the doctor's comments.

"Be my guest," the doctor permitted.

Just then, another knight entered the room, and the doctor left to attend to his injury. Ray pulled the bed curtains shut, then sat down beside me and took my hand. I glanced over at him to find that his fretful expression had now hardened into anger.

"*Not as frail as we imagine you to be*, huh? What a joke." He was quoting the statement I'd made to Rebecca and Mona yesterday. "I understand you felt obligated to honor a request from our Queen, but you need to be aware of your physical limits when you work."

"How was I supposed to know? I've never gotten heatstroke from curling hair before!"

"Because you were living in *Myulan*. But you're in Vaxwald now, and Vaxwald gets hot. You have to be *more careful*," he snapped. "When we first met in Myulan, you told me you didn't really think of yourself as a Flowerfolk. You grew up surrounded by humans, so you felt like you were one of them. I get that. But know this, Mayna: you may look human, but you're *not*."

At this point, he noticed that I was on the verge of tears, and he stopped short.

"Don't yell at me," I whimpered.

"...Sorry." He squeezed my hand apologetically.

He'd been holding my hand an awful lot today. *What are you, my mom?*

THE next day, I felt much better. I was on a walk with the Princess out in the castle's massive front garden. Together with Rebecca, Mona, and Sari, the five of us walked along the edge of the moat and stared down at the fish swimming within. The servants were carrying all the necessary implements to have a tea party in the gazebo afterward.

"It's nice to step outside and get some fresh air," I commented.

"Quite," Patricia replied.

The two of us were holding parasols, shielding ourselves from the sunrays. Normally I wouldn't have brought one, but after yesterday's heatstroke incident, I figured it couldn't hurt to err on the side of caution.

Still, I could feel Ray's gaze boring into me as he and the other bodyguards trailed behind us. I knew he was just keeping an eye out lest I pass out again, but I felt like a criminal under surveillance.

He'd been overly concerned ever since yesterday, and it clearly wasn't an act. So what was going on? Was he trying to be my new overprotective father or what?

As we approached the front gates, I noticed there was a bit of a commotion going on. In the distance, I saw a crowd of people gathered outside. The gatekeeper was gesturing for them to leave, but they ignored him and raised their fists in perfect sync—

"ANNUL THE MARRIAGE!"

"Cancel the wedding between Dario and Patricia!"

The second I registered what they were saying, I felt the impulse to clap my hands over Patricia's ears. Unfortunately, she had already taken notice, and her expression stiffened.

"Our Prince deserves better than that sorry excuse for a princess!"

Thank heavens the crowd didn't seem to notice that Patricia was out here. Perhaps the parasol had kept her face hidden, or maybe they couldn't see through the garden trees.

"Let's get you back inside," Ray told the Princess.

Staring down at the ground, she nodded, practically hiding under her parasol.

"Don't let it get to you, all right? They don't know the first thing about you. They've been hoodwinked by those false rumors, that's all."

"Yeah, what Ray said," Rebecca chimed in. "These protesters are a bunch of idiots who can't think for themselves. They're just a particularly loud minority, that's all. Trust me, the vast majority of Dragonkin know better than to take rumors as truth. Besides, unlike them, *we* actually know what you're like...and we all think you're a wonderful princess."

Patricia merely slumped her shoulders. "I know it's unrealistic to want *every single person* to like me, but...this really breaks my heart."

Chapter 11: A Trip into Town

THE next day, I decided to go and explore the castle town.

Outside of eating lunch with the Prince, Patricia didn't have any important plans scheduled, so I styled her hair up nice and tight so it would last throughout the day. Once I was done, I was free until evening, when I'd return for her nightly upkeep. So I had plenty of daytime hours available to tour the city and observe the hairstyles of Vaxwald commoners. Plus, that reward money from the Queen was burning a hole in my pocket, so I figured I could browse around for some hair ornaments and accessories while I was at it.

Patricia's still really hung up on the incident from yesterday... Hopefully she feels better after talking to Prince Dario, I thought as I walked down Main Street.

Just then, I spotted a group of young girls staring in my direction and blushing.

"So dreamy..." one of them whispered as we passed each other.

Dreamy? Me? No, surely not. Upon further reflection, I realized their gaze was pointed over my head...but before I could turn around, I felt a tap on my shoulder.

"Did you bring your parasol, Mayna?"

I whirled around to find *Ray* of all people standing there. "What are *you* doing here?!" I yelped in surprise.

"I had the day off work," he replied flatly, ignoring the gaggle of girls admiring him from afar.

"That doesn't explain why you're *here*. If anything, you ought to be relaxing in your quarters or something. Or do you mean to suggest you had similar plans for today entirely by coincidence?"

"Yeah, something like that."

How very vague. I quirked a brow. "I see. Well then, I'll be going now. Don't worry, I'll be mindful of the heat."

I opened my parasol, slung it over my shoulder, and turned to go when I suddenly felt a hand on my shoulder.

"Hold on a minute. Isn't this your first time in the city? I'll be your guide so you don't get lost. Besides, there are a lot of pickpockets in these parts."

"Oh, really? In that case...hmmm...I guess I'll take you up on that," I decided after an extended internal debate. Being around Ray was always awkward, but at the same time, I felt safer having at least one other person with me.

Although Ray had seemed rather pleased that I agreed, when put into practice, he really didn't "guide" me at all—just followed along behind me. *Now that I think about it, why would I need a guide when I'm just walking down the street?*

I thought maybe he could help me find the hair accessory stores, but when I asked, he simply said, "I wouldn't know—I've never thought to look." In the end, all I could do was keep walking until I found one, observing hairstyles as I went.

"Dragonkin men all seem to have really short hair... They make yours look long by comparison... And as for the women, sure enough, theirs is mostly long and straight..."

But as it turned out, I wasn't the only one ruminating on hair at the moment.

A group of three young women approached me. "Pardon me, but how do you get your hair to look like that?" one of them asked.

Today I was wearing my hair in a single braid starting from the crown of my head. This was no ordinary braid, however. First, I'd put the upper half of my hair in a ponytail, then tucked it into itself. From there, I braided it into the loose lower half of my hair, creating three small separate braids. Then I took those, fanned them out, and braided them into a single giant plait, atop which sat a hairband.

In Myulan I would've styled it up further, but I had been meaning to experiment with Vaxwald style for a change, and today was the perfect opportunity.

"It's pretty easy, believe it or not. I could do it for you, if you like."

"Really?"

"*Mayna*," Ray chided. He seemed to think better of trying to stop me, however, because he eventually took up the duty of holding my parasol for me as I worked.

I pulled the three of them to the side of the street where we wouldn't block foot traffic, then set about braiding their hair the same as mine. By the time I was finished, the young ladies were beaming with delight.

"That *was* pretty easy! You weren't kidding! Now that I've seen you do it twice, I'm sure I'll remember the steps. Besides, I've had some practice doing Myulan braids."

"By all means, give it a try sometime! Oh, and while I have you, take this. It's the hairstyle Her Highness Princess Patricia wore to her Vaxwald debut party."

I pulled the spare pamphlets from my satchel and passed them out. This was precisely why I thought to bring them.

"Wow... An authentic royal hairstyle?"

All at once, the ladies' eyes lit up. Not that I blamed them, of course—surely anyone would dream of looking like a princess.

"Thank you! I'd be more than happy to take this off your hands!"

"You're very welcome."

"Just wondering, but...are you two a couple? You're not Bondmates by any chance, are you?" one of the girls whispered to me, her eyes on Ray.

"No, no, nothing of the sort," I quickly replied.

At this point they invited him to grab drinks with them, but he wriggled out of it by pointing at me and saying, "I need to stay with her."

Uhhh, you really don't, but okay.

"Awww, darn..."

"Rrgh... I just know my one true Bondmate is out there somewhere..."

As the group of girls wandered away in disappointment, I commented, "These young Dragonkin care an awful lot about finding their Bondmate, don't they?"

"Indeed—and doubly so knowing not everyone is destined to have one at all."

Granted, I could certainly see the appeal of a soulmate, but I couldn't help but wonder why they cared *that* much. After all, if Bondmates were really that unique and special, then would Ray have mistaken me for his? I somehow doubted it.

Unfortunately, by the time I realized precisely what we were discussing, the air between us had already grown stiff and awkward.

Ray pointed at a nearby shop to break the tension. "Hey, look. There's a jewelry store. They might have hair ornaments."

At first glance, the store in question appeared to be entirely out of my price range, but I didn't have it in me to argue the point, so in I went.

"Welcome. Can I help you find anything?" an older gentleman asked as we entered—likely the owner, if I had to wager a guess. His probing gaze was fixed on Ray; perhaps he'd deemed my male companion worthy clientele. I, however, was just here to window-shop.

I really hope the owner doesn't mind.

"Do you have any hair ornaments?" Ray asked while I was busy feeling out of place.

"Right over here."

I took one look at the display case and let out a gasp of admiration. "Wow...!"

The case was filled with luxurious ornaments made of gold and silver, some with jewels or pearls embedded in them. They sparkled under the display lights, dazzling my eyes—but I couldn't see any price tags, which meant they definitely cost a ridiculous amount far beyond my personal budget. *Maybe I'll ask about the price next time I'm shopping for Patricia.*

Since I couldn't afford anything, I decided the least I could do was take careful note of their designs. *That little bird ornament is so darling... Oh, and I like that one there with the tear-shaped jewels hanging from it... I bet I'd look like a chandelier wearing that...*

They were all perfectly lovely...but then I spotted something that stole my heart.

"Oh, wow!"

With no precious metals or encrusted jewels to be seen, it was quite possibly the most ordinary item in the case, but I could innately sense its value.

"This is iridian whiteshell, isn't it?"

"It is indeed... You have a sharp eye, miss," the owner replied, looking a bit surprised that a commoner like myself would be so well-informed.

Iridian whiteshell, as the name suggests, is a shell material harvested from beaches. Normally it's white in color, but under the light, it faintly shines with all the colors of the rainbow. And of all the shells popularly used in crafting jewelry, this one is by far the most rare and valuable.

This particular accessory took the shape of a cluster of small flowers, each petal its own separate piece of whiteshell. The shells themselves were normally quite large, so the designer would've had to carefully break it and then sand the fragments into the perfect size for every single piece. In the center of each flower sparkled a tiny pale jewel of some sort—possibly a diamond.

"These flowers are meant to be miniature *Nemophila*, aren't they? I can tell by the shape," Ray observed as he admired the accessory with me.

Personally, I was impressed he knew them by name. I was quite fond of the little blue blooms myself, but they weren't popular like roses, and as such, they weren't exactly the sort of flower the average person could recognize offhand.

"Why, yes. I'm surprised you knew that."

"They're fairly common here in Vaxwald. As a boy I would always see them around town, but I never knew what they were called until recently, when I finally became curious enough to look it up. Apparently some countries refer to them as baby blue eyes, too."

"Interesting..."

His comment reminded me of the time when my mother told me I had "the sweetest baby blue eyes, just like the flower."

Something stuck out to me, however—why now, of all times, would Ray suddenly take an interest in some common flower? He didn't really strike me as the plant-loving type.

As I pondered this, I turned to the owner and asked a slightly more pressing question: "Pardon me, but how much are you asking for this?"

I braced myself, ready to pick my jaw up off the floor, but the figure he quoted was actually a lot more reasonable than I was expecting. That said, it was still *very* expensive, so if I was going to buy it, I needed to be one hundred percent committed to the purchase. Still, at the very least, I could afford it.

It probably helped that it was made from a shell. While iridian whiteshell was valuable in its own right, I imagined its jewel-studded neighbors all had an extra zero at the end of their price tags.

"This is the only iridian whiteshell ornament that I have for sale, and once it's sold, I can't guarantee when or if I'll get more in stock. I doubt my competitors would carry any, either."

"Nngh..."

I hesitated. As much as I wanted it, I didn't have the entire sum on hand. Granted, I could ask him to hold it for me and return with the full amount another day, but this was a great deal more than I was comfortable spending on an impulse purchase. I needed to think this through rationally.

"I really, really love it, but I think I need to sleep on it and come back another time."

Dying inside, I wrenched myself away from the display case and left the store with the full knowledge that I might never see that beautiful ornament again.

"You sure? I thought you really liked it," Ray asked curiously, as though he sincerely had no idea what was stopping me from buying it.

"Didn't you hear the price he quoted?" I asked.

"Yeah, so? What about it?"

Oh, you sweet, ignorant aristocrat.

AFTER I bid a heartrending goodbye to the iridian whiteshell accessory, the two of us were walking down the main street when I suddenly spotted a small crowd forming in the nearby plaza. There, a newspaper stand had opened for business, and a line of people were waiting to make their purchases. Reading the paper struck me as a good way to stay up to date on the latest Vaxwald happenings, so I walked over—

"Come one, come all! Get the scoop on the truth behind the royal rumors!" the vendor proclaimed.

Frowning, I got in line. Once it was my turn, I took a coin from my wallet and handed it over to the vendor.

"Thanks for stopping by!"

I took the newspaper—more of a flyer if anything—and stared down at it, brow deeply furrowed. Behind me, I felt Ray reading over my shoulder.

Sure enough, the article was definitely about Princess Patricia, but at no point did it clarify that the rumors were false. To the contrary, it was a scathing, libelous takedown completely in line with the rest of the smear campaign against her.

> **"We received exclusive testimony from a Myulan servant who has worked for Princess Patricia for years. According to her, 'the Princess is every bit as immature as she looks. She'll fly into a violent rage at the slightest mistake, and she's been known to throw vases or hit people during one of her tantrums.' Our anonymous informant reported that 'Patricia LOVES to spend money on new, shiny things. You name it, she buys it: dresses, jewelry, furniture, carriages... She'll get bored and buy new ones every other week. She'll even replace her pets once they stop being small and cute.' One can only hope she won't start looking to replace Prince Dario once the novelty has worn off."**

As I read the article aloud, my voice grew steadily lower and lower. Who could this "informant" possibly be? Or was that fabricated, too? I had worked for the Princess for the past two years, and at no point did I *ever* hear of her hitting anyone. We had our fair share of gossip rags back in Myulan; surely they would've been all over a story like that, assuming it had actually happened.

Not only that, but this "testimony" about "Patricia's love of spending" was *blatantly* false. Sure, she was tuned in to the current trends and bought her fair share of new things, and maybe she didn't always wear the same dress more than once, but was that really so different from any other princess? Surely even Dario had outfits in his closet that he'd only worn once.

"Replacing older pets? She doesn't even *have* any pets!" I growled.

But everyone else in the plaza was having a completely different reaction to this article:

"She *throws vases at her servants*?"

"Oh my god..."

It wasn't clear whether they actually believed what was written, but not one of them was openly declaring the article to be codswallop. Perhaps this was only natural, given that no one here knew the Princess on a personal level. They didn't have the details required to make an informed decision on the subject.

But *I* did.

I stormed back over to the vendor.

"Did you write this? Were you the one who interviewed this Myulan servant?"

"Lady, I just sell the papers. That's all I'm paid to do," the man replied flippantly.

"Then who was it that wrote this tripe?"

"One of our reporters. But if *factual accuracy* is your problem, then take it elsewhere. In this business, sometimes the news is the honest truth, but other times, the news is whatever sells." He laughed.

Furious, I puffed myself up, but Ray held out a hand to stop me. "The *Sun Guardian* is nothing more than a gossip rag. Their reader base knows it full well, and as such, they don't take these articles as gospel—"

"I refuse to accept that this woman is going to marry our Prince Dario!" a woman exclaimed nearby.

"...Generally speaking," Ray finished awkwardly.

I summoned up all of my courage and thrust my copy of the *Sun Guardian* into the air.

"Listen up, everyone!" I shouted across the plaza. "Please, don't buy into this muckraking! The Princess is *not* the sort of person these rumors make her out to be!"

I wasn't accustomed to making public speeches, but this was no time to be shy or embarrassed. I fought to keep my voice calm and level as I continued.

"When Her Highness left Myulan, she was forced to leave all of her friends and family behind. She came here with only her hairstylist at her side. She was so anxious about Vaxwald, she broke down in tears—but she didn't let her fear stop her. Instead, this *sixteen-year-old child* chose to put in the effort to form a strong connection to Prince Dario, all for the sake of their two nations. So please, try to see her for who she is and draw your own conclusions. Don't let someone else dictate your opinion for you."

The people in the plaza had all turned their attention to me.

"The royal wedding is right around the corner. On the big day, I hope you'll all come and visit the castle, or even just watch from a distance. Just wait until you see the smile on Prince Dario's face whenever he's with her—that alone should be proof enough that she's not the monster you're all dreading. And when you see her in all her grace and dignity, you'll realize that she's fit to be Queen."

I'd never been more resolute in all my life.

"She's *not* the person you see depicted in this article. I'm begging you, please...don't reject her before you ever get to know her."

By the time my little monologue had come to an end, I was completely out of breath. Silence fell over the plaza. Then, after a moment, someone started clapping. Two people. Three. Eventually the entire plaza was drowned in applause.

"That was a great speech!" a middle-aged gentleman said to me. "You don't look like a politician, but you seem to know the Princess very well... Are you her advisor or something?"

"No, I'm just a hairstylist," I answered.

As I stood there, other people chimed in:

"I can tell you care deeply for Her Highness."

"Perhaps we ought to think more critically about the rumors."

It was such a relief to hear. Of course, I knew it wouldn't be anywhere near enough to stop the smear campaign in its tracks, but nevertheless, I was proud of myself for taking action...and I wasn't done yet.

I took out my pamphlets and started passing them out.

"This is the trendy new hairstyle Her Highness wore at a recent soirée. It's easier than it looks!" I explained, wearing my most professional smile.

The people in the plaza each took one and peered down at it curiously.

Ray smirked as he watched my antics. "I never knew you were so strong-willed."

"I'll take that as a compliment," I replied.

He grinned, then turned to the newspaper vendor, who was balefully watching my pamphlet trump his paper in popularity.

"The *Sun Guardian* has been crossing the line a lot lately. Clearly you must think these libelous articles are what sells when it comes to news about Her Highness."

"Come again, pal? Like I said, I only get paid to sell the papers."

"Yes, and I imagine you'll be penalized accordingly. Prince Dario plans to take action against any publications that write defamatory statements against his future Queen, and the *Sun Guardian* is on his list. Keep vilifying her and you won't like what happens next," Ray threatened, his gaze icy.

A pair of knights rode up on horseback. One of them was clutching a copy of the *Sun Guardian* in his hand. "You there! Are you selling this publication? I must warn you—"

"Crap!" The vendor promptly took off running.

"Hey! Wait!"

But the knights didn't give chase; evidently their goal was merely to get him out of the plaza. Perhaps Vaxwald was like Myulan where the concept of *lèse-majesté* had fallen out of fashion, so they wouldn't be able to arrest him for it.

"Was the *Sun Guardian* the source of all the rumors?" I asked Ray.

"It's possible it was originally a publicity stunt to sell papers...but the investigation has yet to turn up anything substantial. You see, Prince Dario thinks there's a chance it's all a Kazarth psyop."

"You mean *Kazarth* is trying to manipulate Vaxwald?"

Kazarth—a small nation sharing borders with both Myulan and Vaxwald. Myulan had never been on very good terms with them, so I couldn't claim to have a favorable opinion of them, myself. Kazarth was known for tiptoeing around Vaxwald in everything it did, probably to avoid a full-scale dragon onslaught.

"Think about it. If this wedding happens, the alliance between Myulan and Vaxwald will be made even stronger. I doubt Kazarth would like that."

He had a point. To Kazarth, a union between our two sizable nations would make us even more terrifying...but they were probably right to be nervous, considering the marriage itself was almost certainly a deliberate tactic to keep them in check. The little nation had been stepping on a lot of toes over the past few years; if anything, surely they should have expected this result. In my opinion, they had no right to complain.

That said, there was no proof that Kazarth was the true mastermind just yet—but in my view, they certainly had the motive.

"GUESS what, Mayna!"

When I returned to the castle that night to braid Patricia's hair for bed, she told me all about her day. According to her, after their lunch together, Dario had taken her to try on her wedding dress. The dress itself wasn't completely ready, but the tailors wanted to ensure it would fit her before adding the finishing touches.

"When I walked out of the fitting room, he said I looked beautiful! And that he can't wait for our wedding day!" Patricia gushed. "You know, at first I was scared to meet the Dragonkin Prince, but the more I talk to him, the more I like him! He's more open and extroverted than I could ever hope to be, but somehow talking to him just makes me feel good about myself, you know? He doesn't put on airs; he's always frank and direct."

"I'm glad to hear it. It sounds like the two of you will make a happy couple," I smiled. It was great to see them growing closer and closer with every passing day, and I was certain their marriage would be a peaceful one, even if she wasn't his Bondmate.

Once Patricia was in bed, I gathered up all my tools and left the room, followed by one of her servants, Sari.

"Hey, where's Kirion?" she asked me. This was the first time she had ever spoken to me directly.

I glanced back at her. "He's in my quarters, heating the curling irons. I'm going to have him practice curling my hair."

He needed the experience or else he wasn't going to improve—but I couldn't bear to ask someone else to risk hair damage or contact burns. Thus, it was up to me.

Personally, I felt this practice session could have waited until lunchtime tomorrow, but Kirion was eager to get started tonight, and rather than put a damper on his enthusiasm, I conceded.

"Right now?!" Sari shouted.

"In your quarters?!" Ray cut in as he stood guard outside Patricia's bedroom. I hadn't even realized he was listening.

"It's nighttime!" Sari continued.

"This is unacceptable!" Ray insisted.

I shrank back. "What's the matter with you two?"

Obviously I had my own misgivings about being alone in a room with a man at night, but our options were limited. It was either my quarters or his.

Sari grabbed me by the wrist and pulled me over to the wall. "You already have Sir Ray, and now you want Kirion, too?" she hissed under her breath so Ray couldn't hear. "Don't you think Sir Ray is more than good enough for you? How can you be so *greedy*?!"

"Now hold on a second," I hissed back. "First of all, Ray and I aren't like that. And second of all, I'm not interested in Kirion, either."

"If you insist on doing your stupid curling practice, then I'm coming, too! I refuse to let you be alone in the room with him!" she yelled in my face.

"I'm coming, too," Ray added, his expression severe.

And so I returned to my quarters with the two of them in tow. When we entered, Kirion looked at me in surprise, then grinned. "I see you've brought an audience," he joked. But once I was within earshot, he whispered, "Wish it was just us."

I sharply looked over to find him wearing his most innocent smile.

These people are so exhausting.

Chapter 12: The Mysterious Gift

LAST night was such a nightmare. All I had to do was sit there and be practiced on, and yet I came away completely exhausted.

"Miss Maynaaaa! Every time I touch your hair, Sir Ray starts glaring at me! Help!"

"Kirion, focus. Ray, face that way."

All night long, there were *dozens* of little exchanges along those lines. Meanwhile, Sari was glaring at me so hard you'd think she was trying to bore a hole straight through my head. Then, not even thirty minutes later, Ray demanded we end the session because "the room's gotten too hot." On top of that, for some reason he made me promise that I wouldn't meet with Kirion alone at night for *any* reason, even for work, *ever* again.

All in all, it was a rather draining night...but the very next morning, my fatigue flew out the window.

Right as I was about to leave my quarters, I opened my door to find a small, neatly wrapped box sitting on the hallway floor just outside. The hallway itself was deserted, so I had no way of knowing who left it, but the card tucked under the ribbon read *For Mayna*, so I scooped it up and stepped back inside my room.

"What *is* this?" I wondered aloud as I untied the ribbon. Then I lifted the lid—

"Oh my god!"

—and there I found the iridian whiteshell accessory I'd swooned over yesterday.

"It's every bit as beautiful as I remember…!"

I ran over to the mirror, took off the accessory I'd been wearing, and put the whiteshell on instead. Fortunately, it paired with today's hairstyle rather nicely. And while it wasn't flashy, it was still eye-catching, affording the wearer an air of pristine elegance.

Giddy, I took a moment to admire myself from every angle, then rushed out of the room. I had someone I needed to thank, after all.

While I was on my way to Patricia's room, I encountered Ray heading the same direction to take his guard shift for the day. Like a gleeful child, I ran after him and touched his arm. "Ray!"

He glanced back, took one look at me—and my hair accessory—and smiled. "Good morning, Mayna. I see you're in a chipper mood today," he greeted. Was he intentionally playing dumb, or what?

"You went and bought this for me, didn't you? Thank you so much!" I exclaimed.

Perhaps someone with a bit more decorum would have declined such an expensive gift, but now that I was wearing it, I couldn't possibly give it back. Still, it was more than I was comfortable accepting from a friend—assuming I could consider him that—so I decided I'd figure out a way to pay him back somehow. But I wasn't going to worry about that until later. For now, I just wanted to express my joy and gratitude.

"See? I put it on right away!"

"It looks great on you. Very pretty."

It was possible he was referring to the accessory and not me specifically, but either way it seemed he was being sincere, and so I was willing to accept the compliment. He gained nothing from giving me this gift, and yet he smiled along with me, almost as if my cheer was contagious.

"That ornament was practically made for you."

"Be honest—it *was* you, wasn't it?"

"Who knows? It's a mystery," he grinned, as if it wasn't completely obvious. This gift couldn't possibly have come from *anyone* else.

"I really, really appreciate this. I'm going to treasure it," I told him.

"Oh! Miss Mayna!" Just then, Kirion turned up, likely on his way to Patricia's quarters as well—and the next words out of his mouth left me speechless: "I see you've already put it on! It looks great!"

"What?"

Baffled, I stared at him. If I didn't know any better, it almost sounded as though *he* was the one who bought it for me.

"What's going on? How do you know about this accessory?"

"What do you mean? Obviously I bought it and left it outside your door, silly! Bet you weren't expecting that, huh?"

"But then...how did you know to choose this specific ornament?" I asked, perplexed. I was pretty sure only Ray could have known how badly I wanted it.

"Well, you see, I was in town yesterday when I saw you and Sir Ray walking down the street together. I wanted to say hello, but the two of you looked like you were having such a great time, and I couldn't bear to interrupt...but then part of me wondered if perhaps you were on a date, so I decided to tail you to find out." He shrugged his shoulders sheepishly. "After you left that jewelry store, I went inside, thinking maybe I could get you something. So I went to the owner and said, 'The woman that was here just now—was there anything she was particularly interested in?' and then he directed me to that accessory."

"You're serious?" I asked dubiously.

At this, Kirion pouted. "You don't believe me?"

Beside us, Ray quirked a brow, suspiciously narrowing his eyes on Kirion.

I really thought this was a gift from Ray... I guess not. And for some reason, I was actually *disappointed* to learn otherwise. In fact, I couldn't help but hold out hope that Ray would admit the gift was from him. He didn't, of course.

"You say you saw us together, but *couldn't bear to interrupt*? That's simply not possible. The Kirion I know would come and hassle us without a second thought."

"Wow, rude!" Kirion laughed uncomfortably.

I removed the accessory and handed it back to him. "I appreciate the gesture, but I'm sorry—I can't accept something that expensive."

A few short moments ago I thought that I *couldn't possibly give it back*, and now here I was, doing just that. Why was it that I was only comfortable with this gift if it came from Ray? Was it because I knew an aristocrat like him could easily afford it?

"Come on, Miss Mayna, don't be like that. Just keep it," Kirion insisted with a sly smile, wrapping his hands around my closed fist. "It doesn't matter how expensive it was. When it comes to my Bondmate, I'll gladly pay any price."

"Your...Bondmate...?" I repeated, as though I hadn't heard him loud and clear.

"Of course! Don't you feel it? Ever since we first met, I've felt something between us, and now I'm certain. You're my Bondmate, Miss Mayna."

Frozen, I forced my stalling brain to think back over the days since Kirion had first arrived. There was certainly *something* between us, all right. Every time I looked into his dark eyes, I felt a deep restlessness in my chest. Even now, my heart was thumping out of control...and here at point-blank range, it almost felt like I was on the cusp of being swallowed whole—

"Don't touch her!" Ray dove between us.

He seized Kirion by the collar and slammed him against the wall.

"Guh...!" Kirion winced in pain.

"Ray!" I shouted, panicked.

"What are you trying to pull?" Ray demanded, glaring down at the other man.

Kirion wheezed for breath. "That really hurts, you know... C'mon, let go of me... Miss Mayna, help...!"

"*Ray!*" I called again, but no response. He didn't even loosen his grip.

"Why would you invent a lie like that?"

"What are you talking about? I'm not lying...!"

"Are you even really a Dragonkin?" Ray growled.

"What's going on out here?!"

Patricia's bedroom door flew open, and Rebecca dashed into the hall, followed by Mona and Sari.

"Kirion!" Sari shouted as she ran over.

But Ray promptly relinquished his grip, and with an icy glare, he turned and left.

"What happened? Are you okay?" Sari asked fretfully.

"I'm all right. I don't know why, but something I did really upset Sir Ray," Kirion explained.

Personally, I was tempted to go after Ray, but that would sadly have to wait. Patricia's hair wasn't going to style itself, after all.

"PATRICIA, what's the matter with your hairstylist today?" Prince Dario asked the Princess once he noticed the hard look on my face. Today the three of us were going over potential hairstyles for the wedding, and I had presented over a dozen new designs for their perusal.

His comment quickly brought me back to my senses, and I wiped the grimace off my face. "I sincerely apologize, Your Highness."

"Something happened with Kirion today," Patricia explained to him, though I wasn't sure how she knew that, since I hadn't told her about it. Then again, perhaps it was obvious, considering any interaction with my apprentice was distant and awkward (on my end, at least; Kirion himself was acting fairly normal).

"Oh yeah? Come to think of it, Ray seemed pretty tense when I saw him in the hall earlier," Darion teased.

"I apologize for the distraction. Let's go ahead and choose a hairstyle for the Princess." I gestured down at the designs on the table. Meanwhile, the bride and groom were having a good chuckle at my expense.

"Personally, I like this one. It suits Patricia's kind and cheerful demeanor."

"Then let's go with that one!" Patricia declared swiftly.

"You sure? Shouldn't you pick one that *you* like?"

"No, that's okay. I want to match your tastes," she told him, blushing faintly. Dario laughed shyly in response.

What a happy couple.

With the bride's wedding hairstyle decided, the Prince rose from his chair and got ready to leave. He was a busy man, and his schedule was packed.

"I didn't know Miss Mayna could draw," Kirion mused as he looked over my designs with Patricia.

"What, you can't?" she replied incredulously.

Dario leaned over to me. "Have fun with Ray," he whispered playfully.

Torn between "Yes, sir" and "No, thank you," I stared resolutely at him for a moment, then asked, "Your Highness, um...is it an accepted practice among Dragonkin men to prank a woman by telling her she's your Bondmate?"

"Is this about Ray?"

"No, not this time." I stared carefully at the floor.

"Ah, now I get it," Dario murmured, shooting a quick glance in Kirion's direction. "No, it's not an accepted practice...but every now and then, there are shallow, thoughtless individuals who use the concept of a Bondmate to prey upon the naïve and gullible."

"I see..."

"Thus, it's up to you to see through it. You must choose your partner not for the things he says, but for the love he gives you." And with that, Prince Dario left the room.

He's so mature, you'd never think he was only eighteen...

That said, this was *not* a matter of choosing between Ray and Kirion. Ray had long since changed his mind and stopped pursuing me. Kirion, on the other hand, was an active problem, and one I didn't know how to handle.

I sighed and looked over to find him grinning at me. "Kirion, can I borrow you for a moment?"

With my apprentice in tow, I stepped into the hall. I wanted to settle this as soon as possible, and fortunately, Sari wasn't around to "chaperone" us. But as I turned, I promptly made eye contact with Ray. *Of course.* I'd forgotten he was on duty out here.

"Where are you going?" he demanded. Whether he was speaking to me or to Kirion, I wasn't certain. Either way, I glanced over my shoulder.

"None of your business," I shot back flatly. Ray took a step in my direction, so I hastily continued, "And *don't* follow us. You're on duty, remember? And for that matter, this doesn't concern you."

At this, Ray stopped short, with a look on his face like a puppy who'd just been commanded to *stay*.

Okay, maybe I was a bit too harsh just now—but after everything he'd put me through? The concern for my health? The gift (yes, I still chose to believe it had come from him)? Why would he do those things for me if I wasn't his Bondmate? At this point, I was exasperated. Not just with him, but with Kirion, too. I couldn't tell what either of them were thinking.

I led Kirion out to the courtyard, then turned to face him. "Kirion, do you honestly think I'm your Bondmate?"

"Yes, of course," he asserted, smiling amicably. "I never said anything until today, but I've suspected it ever since we first met."

"Then what about Sari? You two have grown rather close lately."

"She's just a friend. But if it makes you insecure, I'll stop talking to her."

"No, there's no need for that."

This was so awkward. We were all coworkers, and we needed to maintain a civil relationship at minimum in order to get our work done. Still, I wanted to make my feelings on the matter perfectly clear.

"Kirion, I can't return your feelings. I understand you see me as your Bondmate, but I don't love you like that."

"That's just because you're not a Dragonkin... If only you were, you'd feel it, too," he alleged with sadness coloring his voice and face. It pained me to hurt him, but at the same time, I couldn't trust that he actually meant what he said.

You see, Kirion was a walking contradiction. While on one hand he seemed like a friendly, extroverted, honest young man...he was also the sort of guy to willfully provoke others and flirt with two women at once. There was clearly more to him than met the eye.

I didn't believe his statement about the hair ornament, either. If it truly was a gift from him, then why didn't he simply give it to me directly? That seemed much more in line with his personality. Plus, the attached card had read "For Mayna." If Kirion had written it, surely he would've written "For *Miss* Mayna" instead.

"I just want to be friends, Kirion," I implored him.

Unfortunately, it seemed he wasn't ready to give up on me just yet. He puffed up his chest, his long dark ponytail swaying with the motion, and declared: "That's not enough for me. I can't be 'just friends' with my Bondmate! So whether you like it or not, I'm going to prove to you that my feelings are real."

"Kirion..."

I'd had enough of this "Bondmate" crap the first time around. I was sincerely, completely, at a total loss.

Chapter 13: Dragons

FIVE days had passed since Kirion first called me his Bondmate, during which he grew increasingly more forward with me, to Ray's exasperation, and I found myself growing more and more exhausted as time wore on.

On the sixth day, Prince Dario decided to take the Princess to observe the knights' training.

The training field was a massive plot of land situated right beside the castle. According to the Prince, the royal knights came here for combat training every day. This was no ordinary practice, mind you; as Dragonkin, the knights of Vaxwald would shift into their dragon forms and take to the skies to spar.

We had occasionally overheard distant roars during our stay thus far, but Patricia's quarters were located on the opposite side of the castle, and we couldn't see the training field from her window. But she caught sight of a dragon yesterday while on a walk around the castle, and she was so enthralled that she insisted Prince Dario let her get a closer look. He was hesitant at first, but eventually conceded.

"I should've said this sooner, but...I'm sorry for making these demands of you, Your Highness," Patricia told Dario as they walked side by side down the corridor. "It was my first time seeing a dragon, and I was ever so excited... If this is against the rules, let me know and I'll go back to my quarters."

"It's not *against the rules...*" he trailed off. It was unlike him to be so hesitant and indirect.

I observed them from behind. Patricia had explicitly invited me to tag along, and I had taken her up on the offer. Behind me followed Patricia's bodyguards, and naturally, Ray was among them. As for Kirion, he had declined the offer, stating he wasn't interested—and personally, I couldn't have been more grateful. The last thing I wanted was to increase the amount of time he and Ray spent in each other's presence.

"Yesterday I was reluctant because...I was worried you'd start to fear dragons and Dragonkin alike, myself included," Dario admitted. "Our dragon forms aren't small and cute like a dog or cat—we're enormous and fierce—and some humans find it creepy that we can transform."

He glanced nervously at her as he spoke; he clearly cared a great deal about his future bride's opinion of him. And as it turned out, I wasn't the only one amused to see this.

"I would *never* find you creepy," Patricia declared with a sweet smile. "On the contrary, I'd love to see your dragon form. I'm told it's quite awe-inspiring, with shiny silver scales."

"Well...if you find you're not afraid of the dragons at the training field, then perhaps..."

In contrast with Patricia's open-minded stance, Dario's uncertainty was downright adorable.

I slowed my pace to walk in step with Ray. "You have a dragon form, too, don't you?" I asked.

"Of course. All Dragonkin have one," he replied.

"I must say, I can't really picture what you'd look like. Are you taking part in today's combat training?"

"No, I'm not. I wouldn't want to scare either of you."

"You're not going to scare me."

"You don't know that. This is your first time seeing Dragonkin transform. In fact, maybe it'd be better if you returned to your quarters instead. I can relate to how His Highness is feeling right now... The second you see it, you'll realize we're monsters, and you'll never look at us the same way again."

"I'm *not* going to see you as a monster," I insisted. *What is he so afraid of?*

We arrived at the training field, where a large group of knights in humanoid form were staring up at the sky. Above them clashed three pairs of dragons. The sound was tremendous—threatening growls, the flapping of heavy wings, labored breathing. It was overwhelming, to say the least. Their sharp fangs...and those claws...

I sensed Ray looking at me and hastily wiped any trace of surprise off my face.

"Time's up!"

At the senior officer's command, the six dragons flew down to the ground and morphed back into humanoids in knight armor. I was puzzled as to where their clothes had gone while they were dragons. Perhaps that was part of the magic.

Another group of six shifted into dragon form and took flight.

"How are you feeling?" Dario asked Patricia.

"Oh, I'm fine," Patricia answered with a confident smile.

From this distance, I couldn't quite gauge the dragons' exact size, but they were almost certainly larger than a carriage at the very least. I could see how they'd make fearsome enemies, but I didn't feel like I was in danger, and thus I really wasn't afraid of them.

I heard Patricia making idle comments like "The scales are so pretty!" and "Everyone has their own unique color!" She didn't sound frightened in the least.

Then, about ten minutes later:

"I'm simply not afraid, Your Highness. Now will you show me your dragon form?"

"Hmmm... Well, all right. In that case, I suppose I'll go and join the training. I haven't gotten much exercise as of late."

Emboldened by Patricia's request, Dario strode off toward the center of the training field...but moments later came to a stop, peering up at the sky. "What's the matter with *him*?" he asked no one in particular.

I noticed Ray staring dubiously up at the sky as well, so I followed suit.

Above us, three pairs of dragons battled at the forefront of a bright blue sky...but one of them, a copper-colored dragon, was clutching his head and shaking it. Did he have a headache or something? He looked to be in pain.

"Is he okay?" I asked Ray.

"I'm not sure... He's acting strange. Stay back, ladies." As he spoke, Ray stepped forward to shield me and Patricia—and in that instant, the writhing dragon's head swiveled around, pointing a vicious, bloodshot glare squarely in our direction.

A split second later, he bared his fangs and came barreling right for us.

He was nearly upon us by the time I realized his target was Patricia beside me.

She screamed. I pulled her into my arms, turned, and shielded her with my body. A token gesture at this point.

If that dragon struck us at full speed, surely neither of us would survive. A chill ran down my spine, sending goosebumps pricking up my arms. I squeezed my eyes shut. *We're going to die.*

But then a roar erupted just behind me. I turned to look.

The copper-colored dragon was now physically restrained in midair by three other dragons. Between them and us stood four *more* dragons—Dario, Ray, and the other bodyguards, perhaps?—acting as a defensive barrier to protect us. At first the copper dragon struggled to free himself, but over time his movements grew sluggish, until suddenly he morphed back to his humanoid form...unconscious.

"What was *that* about...?" Patricia whispered blankly.

The silver dragon in front of us turned back and looked at her anxiously.

"Prince Dario...?" she ventured.

"Yes, it's me. Are you all right?" he asked in a deeper, rumbling voice.

"Oh, yes, I'm fine. Thank you for protecting me." Still trembling, Patricia tottered over to dragon-Dario at once—and the Prince himself looked quite relieved to see she harbored no fear toward him.

Meanwhile, a flamboyant gold dragon stepped away from the commotion and trotted up to me. "What about you, Mayna? Are you hurt?"

"Is that you, Ray?"

The voice certainly sounded like his, though deeper.

"...Are you frightened?" the dragon asked, somewhat timidly.

"No, I'm not," I answered. "Because I know who you are, and no matter what form you take, you're not a monster."

At my reply, Ray smiled slightly (if you could call turned up lips on a dragon a smile), then shifted back to his humanoid form and jogged over to the unconscious knight. Around me, the other dragons were shifting back, too.

Dario turned from Patricia to Ray. "What happened?"

"I'm not sure."

"It looked like he was trying to attack the Princess."

"Agreed."

More knights ran over from the opposite end of the training field. "Prince Dario! Princess Patricia! Are you unharmed?!"

"Not to worry; we're fine. Now then, we need to wake this fellow up, because I mean to interrogate him. We're very fortunate Her Highness didn't suffer any injuries—if she had, we would've had a diplomatic scandal on our hands. The whole wedding might've been called off!"

At Dario's request, the senior officer began to shake the unconscious man. "Ian! Wake up, Ian!"

With one hand clutching his head, Ian pushed himself into a sitting position, groaning in pain.

"Are you aware of what it is you've done?!" the officer roared furiously.

For a moment Ian stared back blankly. Then he searched his memory...and, at last, all the color drained from his face. "W-Wait! I never wanted to attack Her Highness! Please, you have to believe me!"

He explained that he'd heard an ear-piercing screech partway through his practice duel, and for some reason, the thought crossed his mind that he needed to kill Patricia.

"It was completely against my will, I swear it!"

"I understand where you're coming from, and I want to trust you... but for now, I'm going to need to place you under arrest."

"I understand, Your Highness..."

Ian didn't protest as the other knights led him away. Dario and Ray watched him go, then turned to the senior officer and started asking questions about him.

"It's been five years now since Ian joined the knight order. He's a good man with a reputable background... I haven't noticed any suspicious behavior from him, either."

Even the senior officer could scarcely believe what had happened.

Ray paused to think, then asked, "How did he feel about the Princess? Did he mention whether he'd bought into the rumors about her?"

"He never brought them up in conversation. Didn't seem too bothered by her presence in the castle, never made any personal comments about her. And once the engagement was made official, he celebrated it right along with the rest of us."

"I see."

Ray fell silent once more, his gaze focused not on the man before him, but the castle in the distance behind him. I followed suit to see if I could spot anything unusual, but came up short.

"Is it possible he was manipulated by a magic spell?" Ray speculated, his eyes still fixed on the castle. Then, finally, he turned back to Prince Dario, who furrowed his brow.

"I can't rule it out, but...who could manage such a thing? I daresay there isn't a Dragonkin alive who could perform such advanced magic."

Evidently Dragonkin were no better mages than Flowerfolk. Generally they were inclined to be physical fighters, so perhaps they only really needed to use mana for form shifting.

"That may be true of Dragonkin, but...well, I'll look into it," Ray replied sternly.

"Please do. Ian didn't appear to be lying, but we can't know for sure. Continue the investigation and surveillance," the Prince commanded. Then he turned to Patricia. "Let's go back to your quarters. I'll walk you there."

"Thank you, Your Highness," she responded.

And so he put an arm around her shoulder and guided her away with him.

I had expected her to be a little more shaken up, considering she was very nearly attacked by a dragon, but she didn't seem troubled at all. Instead, she was blushing and fawning over Dario's kind gesture as if it were any other day. Perhaps that arm around her shoulder was more of a big deal in her eyes... I started after her—

"Mayna," Ray called.

I stopped short and turned.

He looked at me with his honey-hued eyes and declared, "Whatever you do, keep an eye on Kirion."

"What? Why?"

"Like I said, I think it's possible Ian was being controlled via magic."

"Yeah, and?"

"And I think Kirion's the culprit."

I quirked a brow. "Well, this is sudden. What makes you suspect him?"

"Because I saw him walking down the corridor just now." Ray indicated the castle. "He was in a position where he could see the training field. You notice how that third-floor window is the only one open? It looked as though he'd just left that area."

"Sorry, what? Which window are you talking about? And for that matter, how can you tell who exactly is walking down the corridor from this distance?"

"I guess you Flowerfolk only have human-level eyesight," he mused. "Listen—when I saw Kirion, he wasn't looking in our direction. He was facing forward as if he were merely going about his business. Of course, this means there's a chance he was just innocently passing by."

"Right. I mean, how could Kirion use high-level magic, anyway? Surely his capabilities are no better than any other Dragonkin."

"Do you really think he's a *Dragonkin*?"

"Yeah...isn't he?"

I pictured Kirion in my mind. Back in Myulan, my mental image of Dragonkin on the whole was typically stocky or muscular, but once I experienced Vaxwald firsthand, I learned the tribe had a whole range of diverse body types. For example, Ray was fairly slender, while Mona was short and curvy. Yes, they were *generally* more muscular than humans on average—but even then, Kirion's thin and petite frame didn't strike me as particularly unusual.

Though his quarry was long gone by now, Ray continued to stare off at the distant castle.

"It's hard to explain. He just doesn't...*feel* like one of us. But perhaps that's simply because I have trouble tolerating him. Perhaps it all boils down to my own personal dislike. Still..." He turned to face me. "His hairstyle is nothing like a Dragonkin's. Granted, I never used to pay attention to people's hair until I met you...but I have to say, the average Dragonkin man would never grow his hair out to that length."

Even I couldn't deny that Kirion's hair was exceptionally long. I put a hand on my chin in contemplation. "Now that you mention it, I've never seen another Dragonkin man with hair as long as his. Generally you all seem to keep it closely cropped. But it's not like it's against the law, right? Surely you can't determine his heritage based on that alone."

"In Vaxwald culture, short hair is seen as masculine. I imagine this is a common view in many countries, but Vaxwald in particular is fairly strict about it. Take *my* hair, for example—you wouldn't believe how frequently other men tell me I should get it cut."

"But it's not even that long!"

"True, but the norm here is a lot shorter. The guys all want me to shave this lower part around here so I can *look more like a real man*," Ray explained, lifting half of his shaggy locks to indicate the back and sides of his head.

I laughed. "I guess long-haired guys really aren't as common here as they are in Myulan. The Dragonkin women all seem to have long hair, though. Perhaps hair length is tied more closely to gender expression here in Vaxwald."

"It is. As it stands now, the average Dragonkin would think Kirion was trying to look like a woman on purpose. At first I didn't think too hard about it—told myself maybe all hairstylists grow their hair out—but now that I'm questioning his heritage, *everything* about him strikes me as suspect. Anyway, I plan to go and speak to Torpan, since she hired him. She told us he used to work for a merchant, and he came with a letter of recommendation, but we can't say for certain it wasn't fabricated... I want firsthand confirmation." He paused, a hard look on his face, and finished, "This may well be my own paranoia speaking, but...until I can be sure he's not dangerous, I want you to make sure you're never caught alone in a room with him."

"That's kind of a tall order, Ray. He's my apprentice."

"I'm begging you, Mayna. I'll keep my eye on him as much as I can, but I still have other duties to attend to. I *need* you to stay on guard whenever I'm not around," he pleaded. He gently reached out and touched my whiteshell hair accessory—the one I was positive he had given to me as a gift.

Once again, it seemed as though he was deeply, sincerely concerned for me, and yet I knew if I asked him directly, he'd probably just ignore the question altogether. Personally, I got the sense that Kirion wasn't the only one with something to hide...and no matter what I did, I most likely wasn't going to find out what that something was.

"Fine. I'll be as careful as I can," I sighed. "There's something about him... I just don't know what."

But I was forced to break this promise a mere five minutes later.

IT was just after Ray and I had gone our separate ways after returning to the castle. I was walking down a deserted hallway—and there he was. Kirion.

"Miss Mayna!" he called as he approached, a bright smile on his lips.

After that conversation with Ray, I couldn't help but reflexively take a step back. Then it occurred to me: *why am I taking Ray's side against Kirion?* Sure, he had an air of mystery that made it difficult to fully trust him...but Ray was hardly worth my trust either, considering he'd named me his Bondmate only to change his mind a few days later.

They were both equally confusing in behavior. For that matter, it was possible Ray was badmouthing Kirion purely to ruin his reputation. But ever since I arrived in Vaxwald, my opinion of Ray had slowly changed. His softer side was peeking through again, reminiscent of those days in Myulan, and it was hard to imagine the fleeting smiles and tenderhearted concern was all one big act.

"Miss Mayna? What's wrong?" Kirion asked, still smiling.

"N-Nothing."

"...Did Sir Ray say something about me?"

It felt as though he'd read my mind, and I flinched. At this, Kirion smirked and turned his gaze to the windows.

"I thought I saw him looking over at me from the training field. And then I saw him start talking to you."

"You were watching us?"

"I happened to catch sight of the training field while I was walking down the hall. And with you back so soon, I'm guessing the session wrapped up a bit earlier than usual. Was there a problem?" he asked, innocently tilting his head. To me, it genuinely seemed as though he had no idea...but I kept my guard up nonetheless. How could he have seen us talking, but not the commotion?

"What were you doing in this part of the castle, Kirion?"

"Like I said, I was just passing through. I'm not barred from this wing of the castle, am I? I was just looking for a friend of mine—one of the servants."

"Okay then, why didn't you come to observe the knights' training? At the time you told us you weren't interested, but the way I see you, you've always been the type to tag along out of pure curiosity."

"Sure, maybe that's how *you* see me. But I'm a Dragonkin, and to me, turning into a dragon is an ordinary part of life. I'm not enthralled by it like you Myulan folk. So knight training has nothing of interest to me."

Just then, an idea struck me.

"Right, you can turn into a dragon! Well, let's see it, then!"

"What, right here?"

"Sure! There's plenty of space here in this corridor. Besides, no one else is around." *Time to find out if Kirion's really a Dragonkin.* I grinned smugly. "You *can* transform, can't you?"

Kirion hesitated...then sighed. "All right. I'll do it."

"What?" I blinked in surprise. "You will?"

"Here I go, okay? Back up a bit."

Concentrating hard, Kirion closed his eyes and put both hands over his face. Then his knees buckled and he pitched forward—and in the next moment when he straightened up, he was undeniably a dragon. His scales were jet-black, and as with his humanoid form, he was on the smaller side.

"Happy now?"

"Y-Yeah... Thank you..." I muttered awkwardly. All in all, I felt pretty stupid for suspecting him.

After Kirion had shifted back, he pouted. "I just *know* Sir Ray's trying to turn you against me. What exactly did he say? That I'm lying about my race?"

"I'm sorry for doubting you, but"—I looked directly into his eyes— "I just don't fully trust you yet."

"How can you say that when you're wearing my gift?" he asked, a sorrowful expression on his face as he touched my whiteshell accessory.

"Because I'm pretty sure it was *Ray* who gave this to me, not you," I stated without hesitation. "I could tell from the look in his eyes when he first saw me wearing it. Besides, you'd never leave someone a gift outside their door. You'd march right up to them and hand it over face to face."

"Once again, that's just your *view* of me. Besides, at no point has Sir Ray ever said the gift was from him—*but I have*. Why won't you just believe me?"

"Well...because...Ray was the only one in the store with me when I first saw it..." I mumbled uncertainly. I had other reasons, of course, but they were less concrete and thus harder to express.

"Miss Mayna, please... You're breaking my heart..." Kirion whispered, his brow furrowed. By all accounts, he looked sincerely crestfallen. "Don't act like you trust Sir Ray over me. He led you to believe you were his Bondmate, then changed his mind about you on a whim, remember?"

"Well, yes, but..."

"*I* would never do that." He moved close and pulled me into his arms. "Can't you see how crazy I am about you?"

"Let go of me, Kirion."

"I don't want to." As I tried to pull away, his arms tightened around me. "I could make you so happy if you would just let me. I'll buy you as many hair ornaments as you like. All the other women will be jealous of how much I spoil you. I'll *cherish* you, Miss Mayna. All you have to do is love me back."

He loosened his grip, and I stepped back slightly—but then he cupped my cheek and leaned in like he was going to kiss me.

"We're Bondmates. It's *destiny*."

But before our lips could meet, I quickly put my hand over his mouth.

"What is a Bondmate to you?" I questioned.

He frowned as though he didn't see the point of the question.

"A Bondmate is much like a soulmate, right? You find yourself drawn to them without really knowing why. A feeling so powerful, 'love at first sight' doesn't begin to cover it. They consume your every waking thought, and you yearn to spend the rest of your life at their side. Their personality is a perfect match for yours, and so you get along perfectly."

"Yes, and? I don't need you to explain the concept to me, Miss Mayna. I already feel that way about you. I want to be with you always."

He reached out and took my hand...but I pulled it away.

"I get the sense that you're very self-centered, Kirion. But according to what I've been told, having a Bondmate isn't about selfish desires. You see, Mona has a Bondmate too, and she was telling me all about it."

Being Bondmates isn't about flirting all the time. The love you have for your Bondmate runs deeper than that. You always want to put their happiness first, no matter what...and as long as they're happy, then your own happiness doesn't matter.

Frustrated, I stared at the floor. "I don't get it... Why does Ray's behavior feel more 'loving' than my *supposed* Bondmate's?"

Not only that, but I was dying to run off and go find him—right this second, if such a thing were possible. I wanted *him* to hold me, not Kirion.

"Miss Mayna..."

His voice sounded weak and forlorn. But when I looked up, for the briefest of moments, his expression didn't *quite* seem to match—and then a split second later, he was back to making puppy-dog eyes at me.

"I don't know what Mona told you, but are you sure she's actually found her Bondmate? Because the love between *real* Bondmates—"

"Kirion!"

At the sudden voice, I looked over and spotted Sari rushing down the hall toward us. At first she looked happy to see him, but then she saw *me*, and instantly her expression soured like milk in the sun.

"What are *you two* doing together?" she asked, fixing me with an accusatory glare.

Her open hostility aside, I was quite glad she had turned up.

"Nothing, really," I answered. And with Kirion now in Sari's capable hands, I hurried off down the hall.

At one point I shot a glance over my shoulder just to be safe, but neither of them had decided to give chase.

Chapter 14: Tales of Tribal Romance

THE wedding was nearly upon us now.

"Only five days away? Where did the time go...?"

This wasn't a serious question, of course. We'd been following a rigorous schedule, so at no point did I forget the passage of time. Still, now that the big day was looming just on the horizon, even *I* was starting to get a little nervous.

Patricia's wedding hairstyle was already set in stone, and I was reasonably confident I could pull it off on my first try, but I was still tempted to suggest we do a practice run, just in case. After all, she'd probably want to see for herself how it would look on her, and in the event it didn't turn out the way she hoped, we still had time to make alterations.

But first, I had my daily tasks to worry about.

That morning, I got ready in a flash, then grabbed my hairstyling tools and hurried off to meet Patricia.

"Oh, good morning, Ray," I greeted as I walked past him into the Princess's bedroom.

"Morning, Mayna," he replied in kind.

Inside, I found that Patricia was already awake. I greeted her along with her three servants.

"Good morning," Rebecca answered promptly.

"Good morning..." Mona replied dreamily, a vacant smile on her face.

Sari simply glared in my direction. Either she was still upset about catching me alone with Kirion two days ago, or she was silently blaming me for his conspicuous absence.

You see, as of yesterday morning, he had been temporarily relieved of his title as Royal Hairstylist's Apprentice—likely a direct result of Ray discussing his suspicions with Prince Dario.

Mind you, Ray almost certainly would've included the possibility of Kirion's innocence in that conversation, so the fact that Dario had taken action seemed to suggest that the Prince was unwilling to allow anyone of even *mildly* dubious character within his future bride's vicinity. Instead, Kirion had been assigned a different job altogether: as of today, he'd been assigned his own room in the castle in which to give haircuts to the servants. After all, with the big day right around the corner, the castle would soon be filled with foreign diplomats and other important guests, and it couldn't hurt to have everyone looking their best. As for Kirion, he seemed to accept this decision without complaint.

In the meantime, the Prince had sent a servant to go and look into Kirion's work history. Should he be proven innocent, he would regain his title and resume work as Patricia's hairstylist. But his hometown was located in a distant, rural part of Vaxwald, so the trip there and back would take a good few days. Timing-wise, this meant the investigation was scheduled to wrap up close to the wedding ceremony.

"Your Highness, why don't we do a trial run of your wedding hairstyle today whenever you can find some time?"

"Why, that's a marvelous idea! I should quite like to see how it will look. I'll have time after breakfast, so let's do it then."

"Understood. In that case, I'll just give you a simple style for the time being."

Once I had styled her hair, I left her quarters. Out in the hall, Ray called out to me. "Mayna, did you run into Kirion yesterday? I can't imagine he was happy to lose his title. I just hope he didn't take that anger out on you."

"No, he didn't." He *did* whimper something about how he wished he could stay with me, but I decided not to mention that. "He's accepted his new post with grace, though he was complaining about the heavy workload when I spoke with him yesterday. It seems there's no shortage of servants interested in a free haircut."

I was trained in cutting hair myself, and at one point I was tempted to help, but after everything that had happened two days ago, I ultimately decided not to. Perhaps he would think me heartless, but so be it; I didn't want to risk him misinterpreting my kindness as anything more. Instead, I advised him to set a maximum daily quota for himself and schedule haircuts based on that.

Ray nodded pensively. "Don't let your guard down around him just yet."

What if this investigation proved that Kirion was telling the truth? That he never used mind control magic on Ian? That he really was who he claimed to be? That he was my Bondmate, and he'd bought the hair ornament for me?

No... Even if the first two proved true, I still couldn't accept the rest. My *real* Bondmate was the person who gave me the gift, and that was—

"OH, it's perfect! I love it! And I'm sure Prince Dario will like it, too. I admit, after everything that's happened, I was a bit worried that something might go wrong on our big day, but now I'm really looking forward to it!" Patricia gushed, admiring her wedding hairstyle. And after all the protesters, rumor-mongering, and even an attempt on her life, I could certainly see why she might be anxious.

Still, I was glad this fancy new hairstyle had brightened up her day, even just a little. Finished with the test run, I took her hair down and restyled it.

With my duties fulfilled, I left the room, and Rebecca followed me out into the hallway in order to go and prepare a cup of tea for the Princess.

"How are you feeling, Mayna?" she asked as we walked down the hall side by side.

"Who, me? I'm fine. You're not worried about me because I'm a Flowerfolk, are you?"

For whatever reason, these Dragonkin all seemed to see Flowerfolk as feeble, helpless creatures.

"It's just... Lately it's been getting colder in the mornings, you know? Suits us just fine, of course, but I was worried it might be a bit much for you."

"No, no, it's great!" I reassured with a smile. "I have to ask, though, why is it that Dragonkin see Flowerfolk as frail? I would understand if you all had direct personal experience, but as I understand it, Vaxwald doesn't have a Flowerfolk or fairy population at all, so I can only assume you've never met one."

"That's correct. You would be the first," Rebecca confirmed my suspicions.

"Then what is it? Is it a mental association with flower fairies?"

"I'm sure that's part of it, but..." Rebecca paused. "I think a lot of us got the idea from *Tales of Tribal Romance*."

"Oh, I've heard of that! I forget when, though... Hmmm..." I tilted my head in contemplation, and a moment later it hit me:

"She's human, but I daresay she looks like a Flowerfolk."

"Indeed, she's quite small and stylish. Fortunate, too, because a real Flowerfolk would never do. I mean, you've read Tales of Tribal Romance, *surely?"*

"Oh, yes, I have. I quite liked the one about the Merfolk."

"Likewise. I also enjoyed the one about the human."

It was at Patricia's big debut party soon after we first arrived in Vaxwald—a conversation between two noble ladies, if memory served.

"*Tales of Tribal Romance* is a famous anthology. Anyone who grew up here has read it at least once," Rebecca explained. "There are five short stories, each with a different Dragonkin protagonist, and each protagonist has a Bondmate from a different tribe: human, Flowerfolk, Merfolk, Treeborn, and Shadowkin, in that order. The stories are about the struggles each Dragonkin faces in forming a relationship with someone from a different culture."

"Sounds like a good book," I mused.

"It's really popular. But not all the stories have a happy ending, you see. The tales of the Flowerfolk and Shadowkin are both quite tragic."

"Oh?"

"Would you like to read it for yourself?" she suggested. "I have a copy I can lend you. And since it's something we've all been reading and rereading since childhood, I'll bet it can help explain why we see Flowerfolk the way we do."

"That would be great, actually!"

"Perfect! I'll bring it with me first thing tomorrow."

"Thanks, I appreciate it."

Or so I said...but internally, I was a bit apprehensive.

I didn't actually get my hands on the book until three days later.

"Sorry about that! I hadn't read it in a while, so I kinda forgot where I put it. But I found it!" Rebecca apologized.

"Oh, no, that's not a problem. I appreciate you going to all the trouble!" I insisted as I took *Tales of Tribal Romance* from her hands. It was about the size of an average book—not too thick, not too thin. Depicted on the cover was a woman of indeterminate tribe snuggled against a dragon.

Once Rebecca and I had parted ways, I went straight to my quarters to start reading. With two days before the royal wedding, the rest of the castle was busy with all sorts of prep work, but as a mere hairstylist, I didn't have much to do.

Before I could start, however, I needed to push my loveseat over to the window to get some light—a formidable task that left me sweaty by the time I was done. Then, at long last, I plopped down on the sofa and flipped through the book until I found the story about the Flowerfolk.

"Here we go..."

It was titled *The Tale of the Flowerfolk*. In this particular story, the Dragonkin protagonist was a man, and the Flowerfolk was a woman. As I turned page after page, I became absorbed in the story—and then the next thing I knew, it was over. No surprise there; these were short stories, after all.

All in all, I found it to be a rather heartrending tale, and sure enough, I could easily see why anyone who grew up reading this would worry about me. After all, the Flowerfolk depicted in the story was much frailer than any actual Flowerfolk in real life.

Not only that, but if nearly every single person in Vaxwald had read this, then Ray had probably read it as well...and if so, that would almost certainly explain his behavior toward me.

As I recalled, I had first told Ray I was a Flowerfolk back in Myulan—back when he thought of me as his Bondmate. It was by no means a secret, so I'd brought it up early on to save time. But looking back, perhaps that was the turning point in our relationship. Ray had been awfully surprised to learn I was a Flowerfolk, and while the change in his behavior was by no means instantaneous, it was still there—even if it took me this long to notice.

Still...if I was right about this, then that would mean Ray was paranoid to the point of stupidity. No offense, but you'd have to be *pretty* naïve to take a fictional story as fact, and I was having a hard time believing Ray could possibly be that irrational. Thus, I was hesitant to come to any conclusions just yet.

But what else could it be? Is a Bondmate's love so deep that it forces you to take fictional possibilities into consideration? No, surely not... He'd have to be insanely overprotective...

Someone suddenly pounded their fist on my door, making me nearly jump out of my skin. "*Mayna!*" a high-pitched voice shrieked angrily from the other side.

"Wh-Who is it?" I called back.

But no response came. Instead, the door flew open. It was Sari.

"Stay away from Kirion!" she demanded without so much as a hello.

"Kirion? Where is this coming from?"

"Don't try to play dumb with me! A servant friend of mine told me she saw you and Kirion talking, just the two of you!"

"I mean, yes, we *did* talk..." I answered, shrinking back in the face of her ferocity.

Obviously I hadn't sought him out on my own; Kirion had tracked me down during his break time for no other reason than to "see me" and chat. Naturally, I had cut the conversation short.

"Kirion is my Bondmate, got it?!" Sari snapped, eyes blazing.

"Your...Bondmate?"

"Yes! He told me so, and I know it's true!"

"...Kirion told you you're his Bondmate?" I repeated, frowning. "Do you feel anything in return?"

"Yes, of course!" She thrust out her chest proudly.

I decided to ask her something I'd wondered for a long time: "Are you in love with him?"

"Duh!" she replied instantly.

"What is it about him that you like?" I pressed.

"Well...he's attractive, and he always tells me I'm the most beautiful girl in the world...and he loves me..."

"How much do you know about him? Where was he born? Does he have any siblings? What's his favorite food?"

"Bondmates don't need to know each other in order to love each other! If anything, that just proves it's real!" she argued loudly, and I decided not to push her buttons any further.

"All right, well, I just want to warn you not to trust him. He's lied and said the same thing to me—"

"Maybe he was lying to *you*, but with *me* it's the real deal! I was first— he told me right after we first met. He was just using you to make me jealous, that's all! Got it?!"

"Got it," I replied with a shrug.

"Hmph!" And with that, she stormed out.

Left alone once more, I wondered to myself: was having a Bondmate that important to her? Perhaps she was one of the many young Dragonkin women who dreamed of having a destined lover. Seeing Mona so affectionate with her own Bondmate probably made her envious, too.

Then along came Kirion, handsome and charming, claiming to be her Bondmate—surely anyone in her position would jump at the chance. But did Sari actually feel the love of a Bondmate toward him, or was she just giddy about being special? I didn't get the same sense of security from her that I felt from Mona.

Regardless, I definitely didn't trust Kirion now. Not if he was going around proclaiming to be Bondmates with half the castle.

There came another knock at the door.

"Mayna? Why's your door open?"

I looked up to find Ray standing there, peering in at me. While I appreciated the knock as a polite gesture, it was a bit pointless to do so when the entire room was on display. I shut my borrowed copy of *Tales of Tribal Romance* and tucked it behind my back at the speed of light.

"Hello there, Ray. What brings you here?"

Much as I was tempted to ask him about it, I held my tongue. On the off chance I was wrong and he *hadn't* gotten any misinformation from this book, I would simply be making a fool of myself by accusing him.

Ray folded his arms across his chest. "You met with Kirion, didn't you?"

"When are you referring to?"

"Today, a little while ago."

Whew. I was relieved to know he hadn't found out about the incident in which Kirion nearly kissed me. *Wait, but then...how did Ray find out about our one-on-one conversation today?*

"A fellow knight told me he saw the two of you together."

"*Another* witness? Did we have a whole audience or what...?" I muttered sarcastically. "Look, all we did was catch up. It was harmless small talk."

"I understand it must prove difficult to avoid meeting or speaking to him altogether, but it's simply not safe to be alone in a room with him. We still haven't proven his innocence—and even if we do, I still wouldn't trust him."

"Relax. We were standing in a busy hallway at the time. And besides, obviously your knight friend was there, so clearly we weren't alone."

Ray scowled. "Look... I don't have any proof that he used magic on Ian to make him attack the Princess, so I can't say for sure. And though I may question his heritage, you saw him morph into a dragon with your own two eyes, so perhaps I'm wrong about that too, but..." He looked into my eyes for a moment, then continued, "I've already caught him lying *at least* once—no, twice!—without so much as batting an eye. He's a liar, and I don't trust him."

"What were the lies?" I asked, and Ray fell silent. Still, I could wager a guess: that Kirion was my Bondmate, and that he had bought the hair accessory. "I always have my guard up around Kirion, okay? Relax," I told him reassuringly.

Evidently my tone sounded too lighthearted for Ray's liking, however. "I'm serious. You have to exercise the *utmost* caution. Don't sit in here alone with your door wide open. Try to stay with Her Highness as much as possible. That way I can be there for you, too."

I nodded. "All right."

"Good. I'll be going now—but as for you, I want you to head straight to the Princess's royal chambers, understand?"

And with that, Ray walked off down the hall.

Chapter 15: Wedding's Eve

A single day remained before the royal wedding between Princess Patricia and Prince Dario. The wedding dress was complete, and Patricia was fidgeting as she tried it on for one final test run—equal parts giddy and terrified, by my estimation. She had grown quite close to Dario over the past month, and I wouldn't be surprised if she was starting to see him in a more romantic light—not the volcanic passion of two Bondmates, perhaps, but a tiny candle's flame, burning soft and slow.

"Ooh, I'm getting nervous..." she murmured, clutching a hand to her chest.

"It'll go just fine, don't you worry," I reassured her. There wasn't much left for me to do now except to style her hair on the morning of the ceremony.

In times like these, I could only imagine the massive weight riding on her shoulders, knowing that this wedding bond would make her the new future queen of Vaxwald. Technically I was free to return home to Myulan just as soon as she felt secure on her own, but looking at her now...the way she smiled even in the face of anxiety...a part of me wished I could stay at her side forever.

For now, we just have to focus on making it through tomorrow, I told myself.

Unfortunately for me, however, the next incident wasn't willing to wait that long.

"YOU'VE got a big day ahead of you. Be sure to get plenty of sleep tonight, all right?" I told Patricia that night as I braided her hair for bed.

"I'm afraid I can't make any promises. I'm simply too nervous to sleep!" she exclaimed.

"Shall I bring you something warm to drink?" Rebecca suggested. "Perhaps a glass of warm milk, or some sleep-inducing herbal tea?"

"Herbal tea would be lovely, please."

"Right away, Your Highness."

With that, Rebecca turned to leave. Meanwhile, I had just finished Patricia's bedtime braids and had started to pack up my hairstyling supplies. As for Mona, she was sifting through the incense in order to select tonight's fragrance. And Sari—

"Sari? What's the matter?" Rebecca called as she headed for the door.

Sari was standing a short distance away from the rest of us, staring down at her hands with a hard look on her face. She was holding something concealed between her palms, but I couldn't make out what it was.

"Sari!" Rebecca called once more.

But Sari ignored her, turned, and walked straight over to where Patricia and I were sitting.

She pulled her left hand away and raised her right.

Her fingers were curled around a pair of gold scissors.

Haircutting shears.

Was she going to exact her revenge on me over Kirion?

No.

Her eyes were focused on Patricia.

"Sari, no!"

I tried to stop her, but she dodged past me, her blades closing around one of the braids descending down Patricia's chest at approximately neck height.

The Princess screamed and jumped back, squeezing her eyes shut in terror. Too thick to be cut with a single snip, the braid now dangled half-intact from her shoulder.

But Sari was intent on finishing the job.

"*STOP!*" I screamed on impulse. I could imagine no fate more cruel than to lose her beautiful long hair...and on the night before her wedding, no less.

Fury flared inside me. Gritting my teeth, I put my hand directly in front of her half-severed braid to shield it from further damage.

As a result, Patricia's hair was kept safe. Unfortunately, my palm was not so lucky. For my efforts, I received a deep gash all the way to my pinky, blood streaming down my arm in red rivulets.

"Sari, how could you?!" Rebecca roared, seizing Sari from behind and pinning her arms up. Sari flailed, eyes bloodshot, waving her bloodied scissors in the air—but just then, our backup arrived in the form of Ray and the other bodyguard who had been stationed just outside the room. They took one look at Sari and apprehended her immediately, confiscating her weapon.

"Mayna!" Ray gasped, staring at my injured left hand. He whipped out a pair of handcuffs, slapped them on Sari, left her with the other guard, then rushed straight over to me. "Mayna, you're hurt! No, don't lower it. Keep it raised if you can!"

"Forget about me—worry about the Princess first! Sari cut her hair!"

Still holding my hand in his, Ray turned and looked over at Patricia. "Are you hurt, Your Highness?"

"Mayna...you're *bleeding*...!" Patricia whispered at nearly the same time, staring down at my hand in shock, just as Ray had. "How awful... We need to get you patched up at once!" Her voice shook with emotion as the color drained from her face. Someone she trusted had just physically attacked her, and yet she seemed more worried for *my* well-being.

"But your *hair*...!" I choked in anguish.

"What about it?"

Only then did she finally turn her gaze to the nearby mirror. She inhaled sharply and froze for a moment, unmoving.

As Ray tended to my wound, he glanced at the Princess, then turned to Mona. "Go and call for the knights. Anyone will do—we're shorthanded. Then call for Prince Dario. And while you're at it, go to the infirmary and summon the doctor, too."

"R-Right!" And with that, Mona scrambled from the room, clearly flustered.

"*Why*...?" I muttered bitterly, my eyes on Sari, who stood cuffed beside the other guardsman. Far more painful than the sting of my palm was the deep ache in my chest when I looked at Patricia's dangling braid. I could understand wanting to hurt *me*, but the Princess? What did she ever do wrong?

Thinking back, Sari was the only one of the three servants who had yet to warm up to Patricia, but even then, she had never shown any strong contempt toward her until now. Or had I simply failed to notice it?

"Isn't it obvious? She's not worthy of our Prince," Sari retorted, curling her lip in a haughty smirk. "Making her queen would put Vaxwald on the path to destruction. She's just a gold-digger."

"That's patently false," I shot back. "How could you possibly buy into those rumors? You had a whole month to get to know Her Highness for yourself—or were you not paying attention?"

"The rumors are real. Kirion told me so."

"Kirion?" I furrowed my brow. I could sense Ray frowning along with me as he cradled my hand like it was a precious jewel.

"Yes, Kirion. He says the rumors are true."

"And you believe him?"

"Of course I do. He's my Bondmate. I would never question anything he says."

"And that's the only reason why you cut her hair?"

"Kirion told me we needed to put a stop to the wedding to protect our country. So he asked me to help him."

So it was *Kirion* who gave the order to damage Patricia's hair. My hands automatically balled into fists.

"Don't squeeze your palm like that. Relax your hand," Ray scolded me.

But before I could respond—

"What will I do...?" Patricia whimpered in a tiny, feeble voice, still staring blankly at her reflection. She lifted a shaking hand and brushed her fingers against the severed strands. "The wedding is tomorrow...and my hair... It's horrid...!"

It killed me inside to see her so utterly crushed. But now was not the time for me to lose myself to emotion. Suppressing my anger toward Kirion and Sari, I spoke in a tone of forced composure.

"It's going to be all right, Your Highness. I know how to style it in order to conceal the uneven parts. Luckily you didn't lose all of it—once it's done up, no one will ever be the wiser. Trust me, I can cover it up. It'll be all right. This won't affect the wedding, not one bit."

I knew I must've sounded like a broken record, but I was genuinely confident in my ability to cover for the missing hair. Nevertheless, tears still welled in Patricia's eyes. No surprise there, of course; I could hide the uneven cut all I wanted, but it wouldn't undo the fact that her hair was cut in the first place.

Together we had put so much love and care into those long locks. They were an important part of her self-image. And now, with all that hard work down the drain, her confidence was in tatters.

"How could you do this to her, Sari?" Rebecca asked sorrowfully. "Even if you didn't physically injure her, it still counts as assault. Did you really think you could get away with it?"

"I can and I will," Sari declared proudly. "Kirion said he'll come and rescue me."

And the very next moment, sure enough, Kirion strolled into the room.

"Kirion..." I whispered.

He wore a gleeful smile, his eyes shining with mirth.

"I did it, Kirion!" Sari shouted...but Kirion wasn't looking at her. He was looking at Ray, who stood with his hand on the hilt of the sword at his belt.

"You *despicable reprobate*," Ray growled as he stepped forward, positioning himself between Kirion and me. Looking at him made the room feel a good ten degrees colder all of a sudden. His rage was barely suppressed.

But Kirion had no response for Ray. Instead, he raised a hand in Patricia's direction, muttered a few words—*an incantation?*—and in the next instant, a fiery vortex shot out from his palm in the Princess's direction.

"*Patricia...!*" I shouted. She let out a high-pitched scream.

But before I could move to shield her, Ray had already taken action—he scooped her out of her chair and dashed out of the blast radius at the last possible second.

A handful of knights stormed into the room. Evidently they had quickly put two and two together; they wasted no time in drawing their blades and closing in on Kirion.

But Kirion wasn't ruffled. Grinning, he leapt straight at me.

"*Mayna!*" Ray screamed.

"Kirion, what are you doing?!" Sari howled.

Kirion pulled me close, reciting another incantation.

And then the world around us vanished from sight.

"WHAT happened...?"

In a blink, the two of us were now standing in a different room altogether, with Kirion's arms still wrapped around me. Patricia and the others were nowhere to be seen.

This room was pitch-dark, but I could make out the silhouettes of tall shelves all around us, reminiscent of a library. These shelves held more than books, however; I spotted documents, boxes, rusty swords and dusty shields, as well as a few tools whose purpose I couldn't begin to guess.

Then I realized Kirion and I were concealed between two shelves. Snapping back to my senses, I pushed against him. "Let go of me!"

With a grin, he stepped back slightly.

"Where are we? What have you done?" I demanded.

"I cast a teleportation spell and moved us to the castle's reference room, where no one ever visits." He slid a hand in his pocket. "Truth be told, I would've liked to go a lot farther, but this was the best I could do with an extra traveler and no magic circle to aid me. Still, they say the closer you are to something, the harder it is to see it. So who knows, maybe they won't find us. I bet they're all out searching the town by now...your Bondmate included."

"...Are you referring to Ray?"

"Aha. You knew, didn't you? Deep down, you knew he was your real Bondmate."

"I don't 'know' anything. I'm not a Dragonkin, so I can't say for sure."

With an air of nonchalance, I turned and started for the door, but Kirion pulled me back and pushed me against the shelf. He leaned in close.

"What's the rush? There are knights crawling all over the castle right now. Let's sit tight for a bit until my mana can recharge. Then we'll teleport in small bursts."

"I'm not just going to stand here and *let you* kidnap me!"

Frankly, I was relieved to hear that we were still in Vaxwald Castle. I didn't know where the reference room was located, but surely if I ran down the hall, I'd find someone eventually.

Unfortunately, Kirion had no intention of letting me escape.

"Oh yeah? What are you going to do about it?" he taunted, placing both of his hands against the shelf on either side of my face to box me in.

And then, I realized—his once-dark eyes were now a brilliant shade of crimson.

"You were just using Sari as your attack dog, weren't you?" I hissed, hoping to conceal my fear.

"I'd *hate* to think of what would happen if the public found out a Vaxwald servant attacked the Princess of Myulan. What a scandal! Why, the whole wedding might get called off!" Kirion commented casually. He took my bandaged left hand and peered down at the bloodstain. "You poor thing... It's plain to see you're the real victim here, and yet bodily harm done to a commoner is considered a mere pittance compared to attempted assault on a member of the royal family. Protecting her stupid hair was only ever going to be a waste of your time."

"Not when the alternative was to stand by and watch her lose something she cares about," I growled back through clenched teeth. The memory of Patricia's stunned expression made my heart ache. Perhaps some people would shrug their shoulders and say, "So what? It's hair! It'll grow back!" but not me. To me, that was akin to saying "So what if you got hurt? It'll heal!"

"Perfect." As I grimaced bitterly, Kirion gazed at me with a rapturous smile on his face. "This is precisely the reaction I wanted. This is why I ordered Sari to strike not the skin, but the hair. Because I knew it would hurt you most."

"What are you after? Is it Patricia, or is it me?"

"Both. At first my target was the Princess—more specifically, the wedding. I wanted to get it called off."

"You bought into those false rumors about her, didn't you?" I asked, my tone accusatory.

He laughed. "You really think I'm that stupid? I wouldn't let mere idle gossip sway my opinion of someone." He turned his bewitching scarlet eyes on me. "And it hurts my feelings that you'd conflate me with the average simpleton. I mean, who do you think spread those rumors in the first place?"

"You didn't...!"

"Oh, I did. I even leaked information to the press. But as it turns out, word of mouth spreads much, much faster! Piece of cake, really."

"Why would you do that...?"

"Because Kazarth hired me to stop the wedding at any cost."

Considering Kazarth's relatively small size and proximity to Vaxwald and Myulan, I could see how it might interpret a political marriage between the two as a threat. I recalled a comment Ray had made during the incident with the newspaper seller: *Prince Dario thinks there's a chance it's all a Kazarth psyop.* Evidently His Highness was right on the money.

I looked at Kirion. "What relationship do you have with the nation of Kazarth? Does this mean you're not a Dragonkin after all?"

"I have no particular attachment to Kazarth. I'm not one of them; I just thought the gig sounded fun, so I agreed to it. And no, I'm not a Dragonkin. Don't associate me with those monsters, if you please."

"Wait, but... then how did you manage to transform into a dragon?"

"With magic, of course. Good thing you didn't ask me to fly, though, or else you would've blown my cover." He clutched my injured hand like he was taking it hostage. "I'm a Shadowkin, actually. You can tell by my red eyes."

For Flowerfolk, countless generations of mating with humans had bred the fairy genes right out of us until we looked mostly human, with the exception of our flower magic and sensitivity to extreme temperatures. We had lost the ability to fly and our wings. But the Shadowkin tribe had no past history of mating with humans that I knew of, and so their demonic heritage was likely still very much intact. They were humanoid in appearance, but possessed long lifespans and a far greater capacity for mana than any Flowerfolk or Dragonkin. Because of this, they could wield exceptionally powerful magic spells.

They were few in number, but they had a great love of conflict, and their mere presence inspired fear and chaos wherever they went. Not exactly the sort of people I was eager to spend my time with, if I had a say.

"That said," Kirion continued, "it'd be a piece of cake for any

Shadowkin to simply change their eye color with magic, like so." For a moment his irises darkened, but before I could process it, they were scarlet once more. "Some Shadowkin like to start riots or commit heinous crimes for attention. Some prefer to stand on the front lines of battle. Some like to kill. But me? I'm a little different. I like to take advantage of weak or sad people and make them my puppets so I can control them from behind the scenes. Guide them down the wrong path. Especially when I'm trying to pull off something this big."

"...And that's why you deceived Sari?"

"I needed someone in close proximity to the Princess, and she was the most volatile one. Torpan was a viable second choice. An old spinster pushing fifty with no living family members—she may seem tough, but she's empty inside. Ideal for my purposes, really. But Sari was in a better position."

Torpan had really seemed to trust Kirion, but she'd merely fallen under his spell. Still, at the end of the day, she was lucky to have escaped Kirion's focus. If she'd fallen for him completely, she might've inadvertently thrown her whole life away, just as Sari had.

"The easiest people to manipulate are those dissatisfied with the status quo. The idealists. But with a little effort, we Shadowkin can take control of just about anyone. We excel at deception. Remember that."

Kirion donned a boyish grin. He was both innocent and twisted, honest and mysterious at the same time. On top of that, he had powerful charisma that could easily mislead people, as well as a distinct lack of sympathy for those who succumbed.

A chill ran down my spine. Perhaps I'd only escaped a similar fate because I was actively wary of him. If I didn't have a passion in life... if I didn't have a job or an income... if I didn't have my family... if I didn't have someone like Ray looking out for me... who knows what might have happened then.

"We understand the weakness in people's hearts. But you? You were nigh impossible," he mused, brushing his fingers against my hair. "You're the sort of person who could never steal or cheat, even if you knew no one else was around. Honest to a fault, in other words. Day in and day out, you put in a great deal of effort for which you are generally rewarded, but even if you aren't, you don't hold it against anyone. You left me nothing to work with."

"Are you seriously complaining that I'm a good person?"

"But on the other hand, nothing feels more satisfying than getting a goody-goody like you to turn to the shadows. By comparison, manipulating Sari is hardly an achievement. I wanted you to give your heart to me... grow jealous over the smallest trifles... lose interest in your work... and eventually fall from grace."

"Sounds like you should get a new hobby. Why approach me, anyway? Did you get bored working on your plan to destroy the engagement from behind the scenes?" I asked with a frown. Did he see us all as toys to be played with?

"Bingo. I volunteered myself as a hairstylist's apprentice purely to get closer to the Princess, but then I found the perfect Flowerfolk target. All the more entertaining since Ray kept getting blatantly jealous every time I made a move."

The way Kirion spoke, he made it sound like Ray and I were a package deal, something I found mildly annoying. But then again, it was thanks to Ray and his stupid "Never mind, you *aren't* my Bondmate" ordeal that I had kept a level head when Kirion told me I was his... Loath as I was to admit it, I was actually starting to feel *grateful* that the mix-up had happened.

"So you're telling me your work history with the merchant was fabricated?"

"*Obviously*. Granted, I gave them the name of a real merchant in Vaxwald, but now that Dario's actually investigating it, I'm sure the truth will come out any day now. I had a hell of a time forging a recommendation letter and putting together a collection of haircutting scissors."

"For what it's worth, you were actually pretty good at cutting hair. I watched you work on some of those servants."

"What can I say? I'm good with my hands." He grinned.

I furrowed my brow. "Then...that means you were the one who controlled Sir Ian's mind and made him attack Her Highness."

"Yep, that was me. But it ended in failure, so I was forced to use Sari next."

"What about the time the hair ornaments went missing? Was that you, too?"

Suddenly it felt like every tiny incident at the castle was his doing, and I was eager for him to prove me wrong...but he didn't. Instead, he smiled mischievously. "Of course it was."

"Why would you do that?" I asked angrily.

"Because I wanted Patricia to think that someone in the castle didn't like her. And I wanted to make you upset, naturally. Regrettably, it wasn't quite enough to rile you up."

"You were messing with me right from the start, weren't you?"

"*Duh*. Though, to be clear, it was partially to make Sari jealous. Jealousy makes people impulsive, you see, and I wanted to make her more susceptible to my manipulation. But rest assured, I wanted to corrupt your heart right from the very first moment I laid eyes on you."

Gee, thanks? I'm...flattered?

"Ray was a big part of it, too. I really like him—I think he'd do great things if he ever went rogue. And if his feelings for you grew dark and twisted... Frankly, even I couldn't handle that. A Dragonkin's love for their Bondmate really is something special, you know? It's just marvelous."

Then, out of nowhere, Kirion seized me by the throat—not to the point that I couldn't breathe, but very nearly. I wheezed.

"I figured if I whisked you away from here, Ray would go nuts looking for you...but perhaps killing you would be more fun than some stupid game of hide and seek. I can only imagine his reaction upon finding your corpse."

His lips were curled in an amused smile that didn't reach his eyes. The contrast frightened me. He was a demon, through and through.

"Or maybe I'll hurt your hand so badly, you can't style hair anymore. I bet that would really crush your spirit...and seeing you in pain would hurt Ray, too. Oh, or maybe I should steal your innocence?" His eyes lit up like he sincerely thought this was a great idea. "Well, what do you think? Which would you prefer? The last one, I'm guessing?"

Still smiling, he seized the front of my dress, ripping the buttons and other decorations from the fabric and exposing my brassiere.

"Stop!"

I pulled his hair and punched his chest—anything to get away from him. My injured hand stung, but I couldn't afford to worry about it right now.

"Ugh, this is so annoying..."

He scowled at my act of resistance, then started to recite something—some sort of incantation. I wasn't sure what he was trying to do, but whatever it was, I knew I needed to stop him. My good hand was busy fending off his left hand, so I reached behind me with my injured hand, hoping to grab some sort of viable weapon off the shelf.

As fate would have it, my fingers came into contact with a decently thick hardbound book. There was no time to hesitate; I grabbed it and swung it at his head with all my might.

"Gah!" Kirion groaned and clapped both hands over the spot where I struck him.

Thank goodness for hardcover books, I thought.

On a whim, I peered down at my impromptu weapon—and realized it was a hardcover edition of *Tales of Tribal Romance,* of all things. Glancing back at the shelf I'd grabbed it from, I noticed there were several other editions of the same book, each with updated cover art as the years wore on. The oldest copy was practically falling apart.

"Were you trying to kill me?!" Kirion snarled, glaring at me reproachfully. "I can't believe this! You're no Flowerfolk! Flowerfolk are all a bunch of wimpy pacifists!"

"That's what you get for underestimating us. Sorry to burst your bubble, but we're not as 'wimpy' as everyone likes to think. We can put up a fight if we have to."

Kirion looked at my injured left hand, still clutching the book. "You used your precious hands to hurt someone? Some hairstylist you turned out to be. You realize you're just going to reopen your wound, right?"

"Don't worry. As long as I still have a few functioning fingers, I should be able to style hair no problem. And right now, my hand matters less to me than beating the crap out of a scumbag who insults people right to their faces."

"You *bitch...*"

This was quite the departure from the affable, devil-may-care persona I had come to associate with Kirion. Never before had I heard him use such foul language, and it felt like I'd discovered the real him. This turned out to be quite the freeing revelation.

"Mayna! Where are you?!"

I could hear Ray's panicked voice in the hall outside the door, accompanied by a flurry of footsteps. Before I could call out to him, however, Kirion clapped a hand over my mouth.

"This is ridiculous. How did he find us so fast? Can Dragonkin sense where their Bondmate is at all times?" he muttered under his breath.

"Mmph! Mmmmph!" In spite of my muffled mouth, I tried my best to call for help.

"Are you in here?!"

The next instant, the door flew off its hinges and slammed to the floor.

"That door was *locked*, you know. Can't you Dragonkin take a hint? Tsk..." Kirion clucked his tongue in frustration.

"Mayna!"

Kirion turned back to the sudden intruder, wearing his usual confident grin. "Hello there, Ray. You're a bit early to the festivities." He positioned me in front of him like a hostage.

It was hard to make out Ray's expression in the dim lighting, but from what I could tell, he was downright *enraged*—far more so than he'd been back in Patricia's room. The tension in the air was so electric, I half expected sparks to fly any second now.

But if Kirion had picked up on the same vibes I had, he certainly didn't let it show. "I just thought of an even better idea. You've made me very angry, Mayna. So how about I kill Ray instead?"

Evidently I must've gotten him pretty good with the book attack... but personally, I would've preferred he took his anger out on me. Nevertheless, Kirion pushed me forward as though he were setting me free.

"Mayna!" Ray rushed over and pulled me into his arms. When he caught sight of my torn dress, he narrowed his eyes and adjusted my clothing. "Just sit tight while I end his life."

His voice was gentle, but the look in his eyes was dead serious. He was furious.

"Are you going to fight me with a sword?" Kirion asked, his tone laced with amusement. "Personally, I'll be using magic. Oh, and I don't mind if we take this elsewhere, seeing as it would be kind of hard to swing a blade in here."

"That won't be necessary. Mayna, go stand over there." Ray directed me over to the corner of the room. Once he made sure I was safe, he turned back to Kirion. "This won't take long."

"You sound awfully confident, considering you can't cast a spell to save your—wait, what the?!"

All of a sudden, Ray's body began to expand right before our eyes. I couldn't see Kirion's face from this vantage point, but I could only imagine how shocked he must have been.

"We're *indoors*, you know!"

In his dragon form, Ray could barely navigate between the bookshelves. He spread his wings up to make sure they wouldn't snag on anything, then lunged forward on legs the size of tree trunks.

The distance between them wasn't that big to start with, and so Kirion had no time to run or dodge, much less recite an incantation.

"Guh!"

In a blink, Kirion's torso disappeared inside Ray's maw, leaving his head and limbs exposed. Then I heard the low crunching of bone. *Ooof.*

At this point, Ray attempted to back out from between the bookcases...but naturally, since he was so large, he couldn't help but bump into everything...and before long, he had knocked a series of items and an entire shelf to the floor.

Fortunately I was completely out of harm's way, but still, I couldn't help but shriek in surprise. The impact had kicked up a cloud of dust, and I covered my mouth to keep myself from inhaling any of it.

Once the bookcase was out of the way, Ray dashed over to the newly unblocked window—the only one in the room, and a rather large one at that. Then, with Kirion still clutched in his teeth, Ray jumped and smashed himself through the window, curtains and all.

"Ray!"

I staggered my way over the messy floor to the window. I couldn't risk getting close enough to peer outside, but from what I could see, this room was pretty far off the ground. Perhaps it was located atop one of Vaxwald Castle's many tall towers.

"*Ray!*" I screamed again. He'd gone through the window at full speed—surely that had to hurt.

But then I heard a voice in the distance: "Up here! I heard some sort of crash. Let's move!"

"I'm in here!" I shouted back. "Ray and Kirion... They've fallen from the window!"

As the knights stormed into the room, I pointed them in Ray's direction. One by one, each of them leapt through the shattered window, then morphed into a dragon in midair and flew down to the ground.

"Is he okay...?" I murmured to myself.

But just then, almost as though he had intentionally waited for the last knight to leave the room, Ray flew back up to the window again.

"Ray!" I exclaimed.

He perched on the window frame, then morphed back to his humanoid form and hopped down into the room. "Hi, Mayna."

"Are you okay?!"

His expression hardened. "I'm fine." Then he unpinned his cape and slung it around my shoulders instead. "What did he do to you?" he asked, his voice teeming with barely suppressed rage.

He must've known something had happened after seeing the tear in my dress...and I got the distinct sense that depending on my answer, he might just fly back out to give Kirion another chomp.

"Nothing. He just ripped my clothes, that's all. I'm fine, I promise," I answered quickly. "Where's Kirion?"

"Do you swear it?"

"What? Yes, I swear it! Now *where's Kirion?*"

"My fellow knights have him tied up. Originally I wanted to break every bone in his body and spit out the pieces, but supposedly they need him alive for interrogation purposes, so I left half intact. At one point he tried to run, but I guess the pain made it too difficult to cast his magic."

"I see..." I was relieved to hear he was safely captured.

"We're going to put him in one of our special anti-magic prison cells down in the dungeon. As I understand it, we had to bring in a Treeborn expert to test them, since they're on par with Shadowkin as magic users."

Whereas Shadowkin were descended from demons, Treeborn were descended from spirits. And like Shadowkin, they hadn't mated with humans much, and so their mana capacity was on the higher side. But the Treeborn tribe was a respectable one; they preferred to live in harmony with nature, and as such, they rarely saw fit to leave their forests or wage wars.

After a moment, Ray gently pulled me into his arms. "Let's get you to the infirmary. We should have the doctor look at your wound."

"We can worry about my wound later. I need to get back to the Princess. After losing so much of her hair, she's got to be completely devastated... Oh, but maybe it'd be smart to tell you everything I know about Kirion first. He told me he's working with Kazarth."

"You can tell me all about it later on. As for Her Highness, Prince Dario is with her at the moment. Right now, your wound takes top priority."

And so Ray carried me from the room without hearing another word. He had a stern look on his face the entire time, mind you, but perhaps that was proof of how worried he was for my well-being. And I couldn't exactly protest, being in his arms and all.

On our way to the infirmary, I had nothing better to do, so I decided to ask him a question: "Kirion was saying that Dragonkin can sense where their Bondmate is at any given time. Is that true?"

Ray must've been distracted with other things, because he responded without hesitation: "If you're nearby, it's pretty easy to tell. But after a certain point, I can only really tell what general direction you're in. As long as you're close, though, I can use your scent to track you pretty reliably. Dragonkin naturally have a keen sense of smell, but it seems the scent of one's Bondmate is especially strong for some reason. Makes it easy to locate your personal possessions, for example."

"What are you, a dog?" I teased.

He smiled slightly. "I know, right? That said, there's no scent trail to follow if you're teleported away by magic."

Wait... Did Ray use my scent to track the missing hair ornaments...?

"I really am your Bondmate after all, aren't I?" I asked casually.

At this, Ray stopped short and looked at me in surprise. He quickly recovered, however, and glanced away as he set off once again.

"No... I was just using 'you' in the figurative sense," he muttered. But he was too late—I was already convinced.

Rather than ask him a dozen more questions, however, I decided to focus on the Princess and the big wedding tomorrow. Surely it could wait until afterward.

Chapter 16: A Girl and Her Hair

ONCE I had received first aid treatment in the infirmary, Ray took me back to Patricia's quarters. There, I found Rebecca and Mona, as well as Prince Dario and, of course, the Princess herself right beside him. Sari was nowhere to be found—likely in the knights' custody, if I had to guess.

I rushed over to Patricia. She was still sitting in her chair, staring at the floor with an empty expression. "Your Highness!"

"Oh, Mayna..." When she looked up, I could see the pain of losing her hair written all over her face.

From there, Dario and Patricia listened quietly as Ray recounted to them everything I had told him about Kirion—that he was not a Dragonkin but a Shadowkin, that Kazarth had hired him to put a stop to the royal wedding, and so on.

Meanwhile, I undid Patricia's braids so I could get a good look at the damage. Sure enough, approximately half of the left braid had been severed from her chin down. Angry as I was, I was still convinced we could manage somehow. After all, it wasn't as though the hair had been pulled from her head entirely. With the remaining length, I could still style it up—and once it was up, no one would be any the wiser.

"Don't worry, Your Highness. We can still do the wedding hairstyle like we planned. I can just style it so no one will see the shorter strands," I explained to Patricia once Ray had finished telling them about Kirion.

Admittedly I had been worried for her emotional well-being, but as it turned out, the young princess had much more mental fortitude than

I gave her credit for...and she had already made up her mind.

"No... There's no need to hide it."

Ray, Dario, and I all looked at her in surprise.

"What do you mean?" I asked.

"I want you to cut the rest of my hair to the same length. That's how I'll wear it for the wedding. I mean, think about it—there's simply no way we could keep a scandal of this size hidden forever. Surely half the castle is talking about it by now. And from there, it'll spread to the commoners. So I may as well own it."

In a blink, warmth had returned to her eyes—the fire of determination to spite those who had done her wrong.

"Plus, this way I might win some pity points. I just know they'll all feel sorry for me, having lost my precious hair! Not only that, but if I wear it short to the wedding, they'll see that I'm quite down-to-earth and not at all fussy... Then they'll realize the rumors were false, and they'll all start to like me!" she declared quietly, yet firmly. "I'm tired of constantly worrying about what other people are saying about me, and I refuse to suffer in silence. So this is where I take a stand. I'm going to change their minds about me!"

I was incredibly touched. I had only been her personal hairstylist for two years—had she always been this strong?

Thinking back, she used to be a bit more innocent and childlike. And while she had her moments of naiveté, I knew her to be a smart and responsible girl... Yes, there were many times over the years when I thought of her as strong, but it wasn't until now that I realized just how much she had matured. Oh, how I wished her parents were here to see this... The thought nearly brought a tear to my eye.

Meanwhile, Patricia pouted her lips. "I admit, losing my hair really broke my heart at first...but now all I feel is *anger*. Sari and Kirion had better watch their backs! I'm *not* going to let Kazarth have its way. The wedding's going to be a total success! They'll see!"

"It appears my bride-to-be is more formidable than I realized," Dario commented with a grin.

At this, Patricia seemed to snap back to her senses. All at once, her face flushed bright red.

"Anyway, she's right," he continued. "I think telling them is smarter than trying to hide it. I'll have the newspaper run an article on it... I'll tell them Sari was tricked into doing it by a Shadowkin assassin from Kazarth. Oh, and I'll tell them he was the source of all those rumors, too. Then I'll have them put the paper out tomorrow morning, before the wedding. They may criticize us for hiring Kirion without the proper background checks, but so be it. At least Patricia's reputation will be restored," he finished with a sheepish smile.

"Thank you, Your Highness," Patricia told him, then turned to me. "Mayna, I want you to know, I never would have found the courage to lop off my hair if it weren't for you. I trust you to give me a good cut... and a lovely style tomorrow morning."

Her faith in me warmed my heart, and I vowed to myself not to let her down. "Of course, Your Highness. I'll turn you into a beautiful bride, short hair and all."

"Just be mindful of your injury," Ray cautioned me quietly.

Ignoring him, I began to brainstorm potential short hairstyles for tomorrow.

ON the morning of the wedding, I arrived just outside Patricia's bedroom to find Ray staring at me with his eyes so wide, they threatened to pop out of their sockets altogether.

"Mayna... Your hair!"

I laughed. "Does it look bad?"

"No, no, it's rather fetching...but still..."

With a smile, I opened the door and walked into the room, where Rebecca, Mona, and even Patricia herself all had the exact same reaction.

"Mayna...? What happened to your hair?"

As of last night, the Princess was already sporting her new cut...and now we matched.

"I cut it!" I answered cheerfully.

You see, after I finished cutting her hair and retired to my quarters last night, I decided I would cut my own hair, too. Not quite as short, mind you—just above the shoulders, but slightly shorter in the back to add depth. Currently I had tucked one side behind my ear.

It was actually really challenging to cut my own hair. For the back of my head, I'd used two mirrors to check my work countless times. Plus, my injured hand had really slowed me down...and as such, I was a touch sleep deprived.

"Mayna... You didn't have to do that!" Patricia frowned, looking deeply guilty.

"Why wouldn't I? Does it look bad?" I asked casually.

"Well, no. It looks quite lovely on you, actually. Very dignified."

"I know, right? Not to sing my own praises, but I think it turned out great. So please, don't blame yourself for my haircut. If anything, you helped me discover a new hairstyle that looks good on me, and now I'm completely smitten! This is the first time I've changed my entire cut rather than just my style!" With that out of the way, I continued, "Your Highness, we're about to start a short hair trend all across Vaxwald. It's not something I can accomplish on my own, but with your help, I can. There are bound to be hundreds upon hundreds of women in this country who are sick of dealing with all the maintenance long hair requires but feel they have no choice due to societal norms... Together, we can set them free."

"Oh, Mayna...!"

"Chasing trends is for commoners. But us?" Gazing into her eyes, I put a hand on my chest. "With one first-rate hairstylist and one royal celebrity, we can make our own trends. And starting now, short cuts will be the cutting-edge fashion."

Patricia broke into a big, bright smile. "I declare, I can never compete with you, Mayna. Yesterday I felt it was rather daring of me to have my hair cut so short, but afterward I actually started to regret it...and now you've made me change my mind all over again!"

"You know, short hair doesn't look as masculine as I thought it would," Rebecca mused. "I actually like it quite a lot. Maybe I should cut mine, too."

"Yeah... Long hair is *really* hard to take care of!" Mona chimed in. "It damages super easily, and it takes so long to wash and dry... It's just such a hassle every day! Personally, I'd love it if short hair came into vogue!"

Grinning to myself, I rolled up my sleeves and turned back to Patricia. Regardless of length, her naturally curly hair had volume in excess, so my plan was to give her a half-up style that would look good with both a tiara and a veil while letting the lower half of her hair hang free.

"Now then, let's get to styling!"

Chapter 17: Bondmates

AND so the royal wedding went off without a hitch. The austere occasion progressed smoothly right to the very end, whereupon the newlyweds stepped out onto the castle balcony amid deafening cheers from the townspeople crammed into the garden below.

"That article wasn't kidding. She really did get her hair cut short! Poor dear."

"She's so brave, too. I don't think I could manage a smile if it were me."

"It still looks rather lovely, though! So glamorous and youthful! A very feminine hairstyle, if you ask me."

"You know, I'd never given any thought to wearing my hair short, but now that Her Highness is doing it, why, it doesn't look that strange at all! It's perfectly cute!"

Standing at the edge of the crowd, I grinned to myself. *I know, right?*

All around me, the Dragonkin were both sympathetic to Patricia's suffering and impressed by her fortitude. Plus, they were *definitely* interested in her new haircut.

"Wait... You've got short hair, too," one of the women commented as she spotted me. "It just looks so natural on you that I hardly noticed!"

"Thank you. I'm actually the Princess's personal hairstylist, and cutting hair is my job. Here—this is her hairstyle, and this is mine." I handed her a flyer from the thick stack I was carrying in my arms. It contained a how-to guide for Patricia's bridal hairstyle, as well as my own, plus a few other sample hairstyles befitting pin-straight Dragonkin hair—all prepared in the event that the women of Vaxwald would be looking to experiment with short cuts.

"If you ever decide to have your hair cut short, you can take this flyer with you to the barbershop to show them what you want. Oh, and if you know anyone who's getting married soon, I strongly recommend that you show them Princess Patricia's hairstyle."

"Oh, my! You know, I'm actually getting married next year! That's why I came—to see the Princess's hair and gown, you know, for reference. I'm not sure if I'll take the plunge and cut my hair just yet, but...oh, I do so love having a nice change of pace every now and then!" she replied with a smile.

I had assumed the older women would be more resistant to the new trend, but boy, was I ever wrong. One of the middle-aged women who took my flyer had this to say about it:

"You know, I've always thought it would be nice to have short hair. After years upon years of wearing my hair in a ponytail, my hairline's started to recede, and no matter how well I try to take care of it, it's always quick to get dirty and lose its shine. All this time, I was afraid of what others would think of a woman who wore her hair short...but now that Her Highness is doing it, I don't have to worry anymore. I'm going to lop it all off first thing tomorrow!"

In the end, the crowd eagerly took my flyers until none remained.

Patricia and Dario had received the blessing of their royal subjects; it was clear the people of Vaxwald had chosen to entrust the two of them with the future of their country. As a result, love and joy had spread all across the nation in honor of their special day.

As for me, I looked up at the clear blue sky. "Now it's time to take care of my *own* business."

THE next day, I was walking through the courtyard with my parasol when Ray called out to me from behind.

"Mayna! Going for a walk? The weather's still really hot during the afternoons. You should try to stay indoors as much as possible."

"It's fine. I won't be out here for long. Aren't you still on the clock?"

"I'm on my lunch break." As he spoke, he took my hand and led me over to a shady spot.

"But I wanted to look at the flowers... Oh well. You know, you're really good at finding me. How'd you know I was here?"

"I just got lucky," he replied hastily. "Anyway, after the incident with Kirion, it's looking like we'll have to hire a new apprentice, won't we?"

"We don't *have* to. I mean, if someone really wants to study under me for some reason, I'm more than happy to oblige, but there's no real rush to find my replacement. You see, I was talking to Her Highness yesterday, and she said to me"—I paused to put on my most refined and ladylike voice—"'I know I told you that you were free to go home once I acclimated to Vaxwald, but the thought of losing you pains me ever so much, especially after all that's happened. It would mean a great deal to me if you'd agree to stay permanently!'"

I thrust out my chest proudly, but Ray simply scowled. "So you're going to stay here? In Vaxwald? Forever?"

"I'm certainly thinking about it. Unlike Her Highness, I'm free to visit Myulan anytime, so I can just ask for some time off to take a trip whenever the mood strikes. Besides, when someone tells me they want me to stay, I'm inclined to listen. I just wish a certain *someone* would take a page out of the Princess's book."

"Who?" Ray quirked a brow as though he sincerely wasn't sure who I meant.

I closed my parasol and pointed at him with it. "*You*, obviously! I know you're only trying to get me to leave because you're worried about my health! I admit, your erratic behavior really threw me for a loop at first, but now I've got you figured out. I've read *Tales of Tribal Romance,* you know."

In the story I read, Dragonkin and Flowerfolk were depicted as polar opposites. Nevertheless, the protagonist discovered his Bondmate was a Flowerfolk, and the two fell in love.

After they moved in together, the Dragonkin's strength proved to be a bit too much for the Flowerfolk, and he often inadvertently injured her. He couldn't even hold her hand without being mindful of his grip; he had to handle her as though she were *literally* a flower. Not even flower fairies are that fragile.

But the biggest problem was the Flowerfolk's sensitivity to extreme temperatures. Vaxwald's four distinct seasons were very stressful for her;

she often collapsed from heat exhaustion in summer and was practically bedridden in winter. In the story, Vaxwald suffered a record-breaking cold wave that buried the entire nation in a thick blanket of snow. The Dragonkin were all used to it and could leave their houses just fine, but the Flowerfolk wasn't so lucky.

Worried for his Bondmate's safety, the protagonist kept the fireplace blazing at all hours of the day and night. Each day, he cautioned the Flowerfolk to stay indoors while he went out to collect firewood. But one day, while he was out buying groceries, a sudden blizzard blew in, delaying his trek home. Having noticed that he was late, the Flowerfolk grew worried and left the house to find him...but the winter winds were so harsh that she quickly grew too cold to move.

By the time the protagonist finally returned home, he found his beloved Bondmate dead on the side of the road. The story concluded with him holding her corpse and sobbing openly. All told, it was a tragic tale.

"You don't want me to be here when winter rolls around. You want me to go back to Myulan, where the weather is mild." Framed in this context, Ray's unfriendly behavior made total sense. "Look... *Tales of Tribal Romance* is fiction. It's not real. I told myself, 'He's a Dragonkin; surely he knows that.' And the idea of you actually believing that I'm going to freeze to death was just so ridiculous, I was convinced it had to be some kind of misunderstanding. But when I thought about how you acted back when I had heatstroke...or your behavior towards Kirion...it all started to point toward you being extremely overprotective of me. In which case, it was possible you had started to see *Tales of Tribal Romance* as a cautionary tale."

I glanced up at him. It was kind of embarrassing, since I was basically accusing him of being in love with me, but it had to be done. I was sick of him jerking me around all the time; I needed to get to the bottom of this mystery.

"Mayna... I..." Ray hesitated, his expression conflicted.

"I'm not asking because I want you to date me or something," I continued. "I just want you to know that if you think you can drive me out of Vaxwald over this, you've got another thing coming. I'm not as weak as the Flowerfolk from the story; I won't freeze to death that easily. And for that matter, I can hold hands with anyone just fine. I mean, look at them! Do these hands look that fragile to you?" I held up my perfectly ordinary hands.

"Yes, they do," Ray replied without hesitation.

"...You're just saying that because of my injury!"

"Even if you weren't injured, I bet I could break them if I squeezed hard enough. Besides, how can you say for certain you can endure our winters when you don't even know what they're like? I concede that this chapter from *Tales of Tribal Romance* was set in North Vaxwald, but we still get a decent amount of snowfall here in the capital...and flowers can't bloom in the snow. But all that aside, I simply can't take you at your word. Not after you've already succumbed to heatstroke once!"

Evidently it was his turn to go on an impassioned tangent. "I only got heatstroke because I was doing a lot of work with fire and curling irons for hours straight," I muttered.

"Well, you never should've agreed to do it in the first place," Ray snapped. "I don't care if it was a request from the Queen—with your talent, you should've found some other way to meet her demands."

"Nngh..."

"You have *zero* self-awareness when it comes to your own physical limits. You think you can do anything a human does. *That's* what worries me. I can never trust you when you say you'll be fine!"

I had no comeback to this.

"And it's not *just* summer and winter you'll have to worry about. A good eighty percent of the year will have temperatures in one extreme or the other. And you'll have to endure it over and over. Every. Single. Year. Do you get that?"

With no way to defend myself, I sulked silently. How did this conversation turn into a lecture? What had I done to deserve it? This wasn't what I wanted at all!

Finally, I just couldn't take it anymore. "Oh, for crying out loud! I *know* the summers will be hot and the winters will be cold. I *know* that the seasons will keep repeating every year. I'm prepared for that! I'm going to take care of myself! And I know I'm not as strong as a human in some aspects. I'm not going to overestimate myself! Happy?!" Then I reiterated my point: "Like I said, if you think you can drive me out of Vaxwald 'for my own safety,' I'm sorry to say, it's not going to work! I have a perfectly good reason to stay here!"

"To support Princess Patricia?"

"That's part of it, but there's more to it than that." Summoning up all my hope and determination, I confided, "I want to style hair not just for Her Highness but commoners, too. Going forward, we're going to see an increase in women who want to wear their hair short, and I want to give them all a nice cut...so I'm thinking about opening my own shop close to the castle. I want to ask each of my clients what they want, and then I want to make that happen for them. I want to help polish the women of Vaxwald until they shine!"

As I spoke, I could feel joy welling in my chest until I was practically gushing.

"And I know the job's too big for just one person, so I want to train an apprentice or two, and I want to forge connections with other people in the industry—crafters that make hair ornaments as well as other barbers—and I want to create a handbook full of how-to instructions for cutting, braiding, and styling!"

My voice was steadily growing louder and louder.

"I know the shop and the handbook are still just pipe dreams, but I'm planning to work towards them, bit by bit."

Filled with excitement at my prospective future, I looked Ray straight in the eye.

"So you see, I still have so much I want to accomplish here in Vaxwald. I won't ask you to support it, but please don't fight me on this. I *refuse* to go back to Myulan. Not yet," I finished with a proud smirk.

Ray stared at me in wide-eyed surprise for a moment, then clapped a hand over his face and fell still. Seconds ticked by.

"Uh, Ray?"

When he finally lowered his hand, after what felt like an eternity...his eyes were shining with the same excitement I felt. "I can never compete with you," he sighed, his smile conflicted. "How can I possibly tell you no when you sound so giddy?" Wrapping his arms around me, he continued, "You're always so quick to flush all my hard work down the drain, you know that? Do you know how hard it was to tell you that you weren't my Bondmate? To leave your side? No...I was so hostile to you, you couldn't possibly have known."

"So I *am* your Bondmate!"

"Of course you are." At last, Ray had finally admitted it. "You were right—when you first told me you were a Flowerfolk, I immediately thought of the Flowerfolk chapter from *Tales of Tribal Romance*. As much as I wanted to take you home with me to Vaxwald, it just didn't feel right. I didn't want to put your life in jeopardy."

I was willing to concede my inability to handle extreme temperatures, but no matter what, I refused to believe that merely existing in Vaxwald over the winter was going to kill me. Maybe if I wandered around outside for hours and hours without a coat or something—but I would never do that. Plus, the castle came equipped with fireplaces.

"You're so paranoid," I muttered.

At this, Ray pulled away slightly, then looked directly into my eyes. "I was worried about more than you freezing to death," he explained. "As I said earlier, in Vaxwald the weather is harsh in some form or another for a majority of the year, and you would have to endure that for years on end. When I thought about how miserable it would make you to have to live here, I just couldn't bear to do that to you."

"I get that," I replied, half-annoyed. *Trust me, I got it the first time.*

"So then I thought about moving to Myulan to be with you...but I hail from the aristocracy, and as an only child, I'm expected to inherit the family legacy. Our bloodline has served the royal family for generations now—I can't just throw all that away. Besides, just as you have your loyalties to the Princess, I too wish to serve His Highness. He'll make a great king one day, and I want to be there to see it."

"I can relate." This time my reply was sincere. Besides, I could never ask him to throw away his career, much less his heritage—especially for someone he barely knew. Had he done so that early into our courtship, it would've made me really uncomfortable.

"Besides, had I actually thrown my life away to come to Myulan, I would've been too ashamed to face you. Perhaps I could find a different job soon enough, but even then...I don't want to disgrace myself in front of you if I can help it." He pulled me back into his arms, more tightly this time. "You can't know how bad it hurt to force myself to leave you. I had to tell myself it was for your own good or else I couldn't have managed it. And yet...despite my noble sacrifice, you turned up in Vaxwald as part of Her Highness's dowry..." Ray grumbled.

"That wasn't my choice! She asked me to come with her!" I argued.

"Do I send you back to Myulan, or do I support your dream...? I just don't know," he muttered, burying his face in my shoulder. Soon, however, it became apparent that he'd found his answer. "In my head, I know the correct answer is to send you home, but you just look so happy when you're talking about your dreams here in Vaxwald...and I can't just turn a blind eye to my Bondmate's feelings. I *can't*."

I stayed quiet and let him work it out for himself.

"When I left Myulan, it was easier. You didn't have strong feelings for me, so my absence didn't pain you."

"If I cried and begged you not to go, would you have stayed?"

"Well, if you were serious about it, then yes, I imagine I would have. Probably would've left my family name and my title to people I could trust. Likewise, I can't exactly disregard your wishes this time around, either. I know you're serious about making your dreams come true, and my only option is to support you."

"Thank you," I said with a smile.

He laughed and straightened up. "When you're having fun, I have fun. When you're happy, I'm happy. And if I'm being honest, I would do anything for you."

"What if I wanted to hike up a snowy mountain?" I teased.

"I would stop you, obviously," he answered with a grin. "But if you honestly, sincerely, *desperately* wanted to go, then I'm sure I'd end up caving eventually. And if we did end up going, I would take *every single precaution* to ensure you won't freeze to death."

"Well, fortunately for you, I don't have a burning desire to hike up a snowy mountain at the moment."

Unless I hear of any rumors that mountain-dwellers have especially healthy hair or unique hairstyles or something like that. Then all bets are off.

"Anyway...I just wish you would've been honest with me right from the start. You should've just told me you were worried about how a Flowerfolk would fare in Vaxwald. Then you wouldn't have pissed me off the way you did." I scowled slightly.

"And so what if I ended up in Vaxwald? Instead of telling me to 'get out,' you should've just cautioned me against the extreme weather conditions so I could make my own informed decision."

"Even if I had, would you have chosen to leave?"

"...Well, no... I came here to support the Princess," I mumbled.

"I knew better than to try to talk it out with you because I knew you weren't fully conscious of your weak constitution," Ray explained, his arms still wrapped around me. "Even now, you think I'm simply 'paranoid' or what have you. Had I been straightforward with you, you would've merely laughed it off."

At this, I stayed silent...because I knew he was right.

"And I only lied about you not being my Bondmate because I felt it was the right thing to do. If I continued to let you think I was a good man, it might have hurt you more when I left you."

"*Somebody's* full of himself," I snarked...but he simply grinned as if to suggest he knew *precisely* how good-looking he was.

"Oh, please. Be honest—after five days together, you were already interested in me, weren't you? Any time I drew close to you or smiled at you, you'd always turn red...right here." He grinned as his fingers brushed my ear.

"Grrr! Quit teasing me!" I growled, embarrassed (and blushing) but not actually annoyed with him.

"I'm not teasing you. It's just cute, that's all." Then his tone turned serious. "I'm sorry I upset you. I just thought it'd be best if I made myself into the bad guy before I left Myulan. And I admit, I've been acting coldly toward you here in Vaxwald because I hoped it would encourage you to go home. I *wanted* to piss you off."

"Too bad for you, I'm not the rage-quitting type. I'm far more professional than that."

"You're right. I was naïve, and I underestimated your devotion to your work." His expression shifted to a confident smile. "So, seeing as you initiated this conversation, can I take this to mean you're ready for what happens next?"

"What do you mean...?" His bright smile put me on guard.

"You made me admit that you're my Bondmate. Then you told me about your ambitions for the future and asked me not to fight it. Thus, my only option is to accept that you're my Bondmate, love you with all my heart, and support you as you work toward your dream."

"I mean, that's not your *only* option," I mumbled shyly.

A big grin crept up on his face. "I'm warning you now: a Dragonkin's love for his Bondmate is rather intense. And I'm done holding back."

Suddenly, it felt as though I had inadvertently awoken a sleeping dragon...and my smile stiffened as I realized there would be no escape...

Chapter 18: Epilogue

WINTER had arrived in full force. I remember wondering to myself back in autumn how the weather could possibly get any colder. What a fool I was.

Ray was right. I was clearly not cut out for Vaxwald winters. Fortunately, having a fireplace made life bearable...as long as I didn't go outside more than was absolutely necessary.

I'd been meaning to scope out a potential location for my future shop, but I knew Ray would yell at me if I tried to go into town by myself, so I decided that it would have to wait. This loss of independence grated on me, but I had no choice. I couldn't very well put myself in danger, after all.

Thankfully, I had a formidable roster of allies on my side: thick blankets, fur coats, gloves, winter hats, scarves, boots, cold-resistant dresses and singlets, and much, much more—all gifts from Ray.

I was walking down the castle corridor wearing a thick shawl when I heard him call out to me. "Mayna!"

(Fun fact: He bought me this shawl, too. Not that I asked him to, but since he wanted me to have it, I figured I may as well use it.)

"Hi, Ray. Is your shift over already?"

"Yeah, I'm done for the day. What about you?"

"Her Highness said she'd have Rebecca do her bedtime braids, so I'm free for the rest of the day. Maybe the Prince told her you were getting off work early. Either way, it was a kind gesture."

As I spoke, Ray gazed at me, smiling softly. He seemed to radiate love from every inch of his body. Nothing out of the ordinary for him these days, of course. We saw each other multiple times a day, and yet he always looked at me like I'm his favorite thing in the world. It made me blush.

"Sounds like we get to go home and eat dinner together." He stroked my hair affectionately.

I was now living at his family estate. Ray claimed it's only proper, seeing as we'll be husband and wife someday, but I suspect he's just afraid I might freeze to death in my bed if I stayed in the castle.

No longer was he assigned to guard Princess Patricia; he'd gone back to serving as bodyguard for Prince Dario. That said, because he sometimes got assigned to the nightshift, his work hours were always a mixed bag, and we seldom went to work or home at the same time.

Fortunately, Ray's family sent a carriage for me whenever I needed to travel by myself, so I wouldn't be freezing to death on the side of the road anytime soon. Personally, I felt bad for imposing on them so much, but they had already remodeled the carriage interior with fur for added cold resistance, so at this point I'd feel worse saying no.

"Your hair's getting longer," Ray commented, wrapping an arm around me and planting a kiss on my forehead. Once he admitted that I was his Bondmate, he became much more openly affectionate; it's something I've had to get used to (because I've learned I can't fight him on it).

"Do you prefer it long? Should I keep growing it out?"

"I like your hair at all lengths. Right now, I think it looks best just the way it is...and whether you grow it out or cut it shorter, I'm sure I'll say the same thing. Trust me, I'm not the person you want to ask those sorts of questions. Same with clothes."

"Tell me about it." Seriously, he was no help at all...but then again, I liked hearing that I'm fine the way I am.

He took my left hand in his. The wound had healed, but in its place it had left a scar. "Are you cold? Your fingers feel a bit chilly."

"Freezing, actually. They really ought to install torches in the halls. I'm fine, though. It won't kill me."

"Are you sure? You look miserable." He paused to kiss my scar, then continued, "Maybe you need to wear more layers. I'm told it's normal to wear multiple singlets at a time."

"Any more layers and I won't be able to extend my arms! Plus, I'll look fat!"

"So what if you look fat? I don't care at all." He paused for a moment...and his expression turned severe. "Or are you trying to look good for someone in particular? Another man?"

"No, of course not!" I replied hastily. Unfortunately, this apparently struck Ray as suspicious, and he narrowed his eyes at me. The silence was so oppressive, I couldn't take it. "I'm serious! I'm not lying to you!"

Unfortunately, the more I said, the faker I sounded.

"If you were to fall in love with someone else, I suppose I ought to support it," he mused, my hand still in his. "I couldn't very well call you my Bondmate if I didn't put your happiness first."

"I'm telling you, there isn't another man!"

"The problem is, I just don't think I could. Maybe if he proved he could love you and care for you better than I could—but I'm confident no one can."

"Full of yourself as always," I teased. He grinned.

"I'm your Bondmate, after all—the only one you're ever going to get. And no one could possibly love you more than your Bondmate."

He pulled me into his arms. *Is he afraid that he'll die if he isn't touching some part of me at all times?* Not that I was opposed to it, of course.

"Tell me you love me."

"What?" For a moment, I failed to process this. It was just such a lovesick teenager thing to say.

Embarrassed, Ray buried his face in my shoulder. "I'm scared that I'm being too forward with you. First I told you that I want to marry you someday, then I made you move to my family's estate... You didn't really get the opportunity to decide for yourself. Not that I wanted you to say no, of course, but...I can't help but worry that you don't love me the way I love you."

"You're actually worried about that?" I murmured, slightly taken aback.

Then again...thinking back, I couldn't recall having ever told him how I felt. Any time he told me he loved me, I would always just thank him and leave it at that.

I stepped out of his embrace and looked him in the eyes.

"Contrary to what others may think, I wouldn't date someone I wasn't interested in, much less move into their parents' house. I have feelings for you, so I've made you part of my life. I love your sweet side—your borderline paranoia over me, your enthusiasm about my dreams, even your smile. I love your soft, warm smile, and I love the playful, mischievous smile you wear whenever you tease me. Oh, and I love your dragon form, too. It's actually kind of cute."

Grinning, I reached up and caressed his blond hair.

"Plus, I love your hair. It's got such a lovely warm golden color to it... but most of all, it's so nice and soft! Very fine and silky. Turns out I like to touch your hair just as much as you like to touch mine."

At this point, Ray was starting to turn red. I lowered my hand.

"I'm in love with you, Ray. Madly in love with you. I'm glad I got to spend time with you here in Vaxwald and discover all your good points." I paused. "Wow, you're really blushing."

"And whose fault is that?!"

"You're the one who told me to tell you I love you!"

He seemed embarrassed and happy and touched, all at the same time.

"I admit, I wasn't always glad you came to Vaxwald, but I am now. Back in Myulan it was essentially love at first sight, but your strong-willed passion for your work made me fall for you all over again. My love grows deeper with every new thing I learn about you." He paused to look away shyly. "Quit staring at me, would you?"

"Sorry, it's just... I've never seen you blush before!"

"In that case, I think it's time I got even."

Putting a hand over my eyes, he leaned in and pressed his lips to mine. After a lengthy exchange, sure enough, I was left blushing even harder.

Ray grinned smugly. "That's better."

And as loath as I am to admit it, I love that smug grin of his, too.

Mona's Observation Log

MY name is Mona, and I work as a servant at Vaxwald Castle. Not only that, but I get to serve the Princess! What an honor!

"Is it fair for one girl to be so blessed?"

As I walked down the corridor, carrying a set of new sheets and pillow covers for Her Highness's bed, I peered through the windows at the bright blue sky. I loved my job, and what's more, fate had seen fit to give me a Bondmate in the form of a man named Padell. I was blessed in every sense of the word.

To an outside observer, Padell probably seemed like an average guy—no big ambitions and nothing much going for him outside of his job as a knight. But to me, he was everything I could ever want. I loved his droopy eyebrows and big, round eyes...but more than anything, I loved his personality.

From the moment we first laid eyes on each other, we knew we were Bondmates, so there was never any need to hesitate and wonder if he liked me back. Naturally, we started dating right away—I mean, why wouldn't we? It's destiny! That's how it is for all Bondmate couples, right?

"Oh... Except for her, I guess..."

Ahead of me, I spotted the one exception to this rule: Mayna, the Princess's personal hairstylist. She had just recently cut her hair short, and it looked great.

"Mayna!" I called, and her beautiful blue eyes shifted in my direction. "Did you finish styling Her Highness's hair?"

"I did. Right now Rebecca's helping her get dressed."

"Okay then, I'll go change her sheets."

But before I could take more than a few steps, I heard someone else's footsteps behind me, so I stopped and turned back.

"Oh! Good day, Your Highness!"

I hastily stepped back against the wall and bowed my head in deference. Prince Dario had arrived, accompanied by Sir Ray and his other bodyguards. Before they reached me, however, they stopped beside Mayna, who was bowing along with me.

"I'm looking forward to Patricia's hairstyle today," said the Prince.

"You won't be disappointed, Your Highness. It'll pair perfectly with that dress you gave her," Mayna replied confidently, and Prince Dario grinned.

"See you at lunch," Sir Ray told her as the group marched on down the hall. Aww, just look at that lovey-dovey smile!

The Ray I knew was easy on the eyes, but at the same time, he had the stalwart determination of a battle-weathered soldier. That's a Dragonkin for you, I guess. But whenever Mayna was around? Suddenly he was all smiles and laughter...almost like an entirely different person! I mean, look at that—one "See you then" from Mayna and he's practically on cloud nine!

Still, I'm ever so glad it's worked out between them. It was so obnoxious—er, uncomfortable—hearing him deny that Mayna was his Bondmate. Watching him really made me angry—I mean, worried!

Early on, I noticed that whenever Mayna wasn't looking, Sir Ray would bite his lip and shoot her these wistful, longing gazes. But now they're finally together, so I don't have to spend every day wishing I could stab—I mean, help them!

Witnessing their little exchange made me long to see Padell. And lunchtime felt like an eternity away.

AT last, lunchtime was upon us. Carrying a gingham basket full of sandwiches I had personally prepared myself, I headed off to find Padell.

Spring had rolled around, bringing with it pleasant warm weather that melted the snow away. As I was contemplating whether to eat outside for a change, I spotted Mayna and Sir Ray sitting on a bench in the courtyard, smiling and chatting.

"You seem kind of down," Sir Ray commented. "Is something wrong?"

Meanwhile, I came to a stop a short distance away so I could eavesdrop. I mean, after all the emotional investment I've put into their relationship, who wouldn't be curious? Fortunately I was positioned directly behind them, so they didn't see me.

Mayna turned to Sir Ray, her eyes wide. "How did you know? I was doing my best to act normal!"

"I always pay close attention to you, so it's easy to tell when something's off. You were perfectly normal when I saw you this morning—what happened?"

Mayna sighed. Apparently she realized there was no use in trying to hide anything from her Bondmate. "Well... You know Lady Iris, the daughter of the Marquess?"

"Yeah, I know her."

"A while back she approached me directly, claiming she wanted to join the short hair trend, and she wanted *me* to do it since everyone's been talking about me. And her appointment was scheduled for this morning."

"How'd it go?"

"Well, I cut her hair...but she didn't like it. 'Was this the best you could do? I had higher hopes than that. I guess the rumors about you were wrong.'"

"She said that to you?"

"Yeah. I'm not that upset about the last part... I just wish she would've liked her haircut." Mayna slumped her shoulders. "But I can't undo what I've done, and now she'll have to live with a haircut she hates, day in and day out, until it grows out again. It's my job to make these women sparkle, so I feel as though I've failed her... I thought I gave her the perfect cut, but...now I'm not so sure..."

"Oh, Mayna..." Sir Ray frowned, sharing in her pain. Silence fell. Then, after a long moment, he put his hand on her shoulder. "Okay, well, what if you tried styling her new hair a different way? If she doesn't like it as-is, maybe the two of you can find a style she *does* like! That's more your area of expertise, is it not?" He smiled. "Don't worry. Just be confident! To me, you're the best stylist this world has to offer. No one's got talent like yours! I'm sure you'll find a way to make her happy again!"

Mayna smiled in spite of herself. "Thank you, but I really don't think I'm the best stylist in the whole world. You compliment me so much, sometimes it can be hard to believe you actually mean it...but at the very least, it always inspires me to have confidence and courage. You're always there to encourage me whenever I need it the most."

She shifted slightly, and I couldn't quite see what she was doing, but I figured she must've taken his hand in hers, because he smiled softly. "Mayna..."

But just when the mood in the air had taken a turn for the romantic, Mayna suddenly relinquished her grip on Ray's hand. "You know, if we're being honest, I was thinking something along those lines myself! I can't just shrug my shoulders and give up! I need to ask her to let me try again!" She leapt to her feet. "I know I can make her look cute with short hair! I want her to smile at herself every time she looks in the mirror! Thank you so much, Ray. I gotta go brainstorm some hairstyles for her!"

And with that, Mayna was gone. Not even her handsome Bondmate could distract her from her deep passion for her work. Personally, I was glad to see her back to her usual self, but at the same time, Sir Ray looked so lonely, left behind on the bench like an abandoned puppy...

It was actually kind of funny. He could've had his pick of the women, and yet fate chose Mayna the workaholic to be his Bondmate. Poor guy... Hang in there, Sir Ray!

With that silent prayer, I hurried off to find Padell.

THE next day, I was walking down the corridor when I spotted Sir Ray yet again. He must've been on the clock, because he was with a fellow knight. When the two of them reached the covered walkway, however, Sir Ray turned to his associate and said, "Actually, there's something important I've forgotten to take care of. Could you go on without me?"

"Alright then."

Once the other knight was gone, Sir Ray glanced over at the woman approaching from up ahead. It was Lady Iris, the aristocrat Mayna had mentioned yesterday, wearing an extravagant dress. And sure enough, her hair was very short...but she was wearing a large, stylish flower ornament that suited her perfectly. In fact, she looked to be on the very cutting edge of the trend. It wasn't a look people with round faces (like me) could pull off, but with her slender figure and high cheekbones, she was *the pinnacle of elegance.*

"Oh wow..."

"She's gorgeous..."

Lady Iris smiled as the servants nearby all swooned in admiration. Puffing out her chest, she strutted down the walkway—that is, until she noticed Sir Ray looking at her.

"Why, hello, Sir Ray," she greeted him.

At this, Sir Ray donned a perfunctory, cordial smile quite unlike the way he'd smile around Mayna. "Hello there. I'm told Mayna cut your hair recently. It looks wonderful."

"Hee hee. It does, doesn't it? I'm glad I decided to take the plunge. Now I turn heads everywhere I go!"

"That's strange. I'd heard you weren't a fan of your new cut."

Lady Iris smiled mischievously. "Oh, she told you? I was lying."

Sir Ray furrowed his brows slightly. "Why would you lie about that?"

She shrugged. "That woman has all the luck. I wanted to take her down a peg."

"What do you mean, she has all the luck?"

"She was chosen to be your Bondmate, was she not? That alone is proof enough! Surely dozens of women out there are wishing it could have been them instead."

Was she one of them? I admit, there was a point in time (before I met Padell) that I thought Sir Ray was totally dreamy... It didn't last long, though. I wasn't too serious about it.

Lady Iris quirked a brow and scoffed. "And yet that honor went to some *hairstylist* from Myulan. She's not even a Dragonkin! So yeah, I wanted to put her in her place. I'm sure she'll get over it."

At this point, I was expecting Sir Ray to knock her off her high horse, but surprisingly, he kept smiling.

"Please don't treat her like that. She never asked for this." Just then, his humble tone grew steely, and the light left his eyes. "And if you hurt my Bondmate, I will personally see to it that you suffer for your misdeeds."

Lady Iris froze. Honestly, I'm not sure what she was expecting. If anyone messed with my Padell, I'd probably try to get revenge, too.

But it was clear Sir Ray wanted to solve things peaceably for Mayna's sake, because he smiled and continued, "That hairstyle really does suit you, by the way. Absolutely stunning."

But while it was obvious from his tone and body language what he really meant—"*Mayna's handiwork* is absolutely stunning"—Lady Iris seemed to think he was referring to her directly.

"Y-Yes, I know," she replied, blushing. "I like it quite a bit. I've been getting so many envious compliments—why, I feel like a new woman."

"In that case, could you at least tell Mayna you've changed your mind?"

"...Very well, if you insist." It was clear she didn't want to get on his bad side. But then she said, "To be clear, I was always going to tell her. Honest. I'm going to need her to cut my hair again, anyway. She's just so passionate about her work... When it comes to hair, it's obvious she really knows her stuff. I couldn't have gotten a better cut from anyone else." She twirled a strand around her finger. "Besides, I was on my way to see her just now. She wanted me to stop by so she could show me some different ways to style it."

At this, Sir Ray frowned. "She never did come to bed last night, did she...?" he muttered under his breath. I'd forgotten they were living together.

Mayna must've been worried sick, thinking Lady Iris was heartbroken over her new cut. She probably stayed up all night long brainstorming hairstyles in order to find a solution as quickly as possible... She did seem sleepy when I saw her this morning...

I snapped back to reality in time to notice Lady Iris strutting off down the hallway. Then Sir Ray looked in my direction. "Oh, Mona. Didn't know you were there. You heard all that?"

I flinched. "Yeah... I got nosy and started eavesdropping. I'm sorry." Ugh, why did I admit to that?! I'm so stupid.

Fortunately for me, Sir Ray didn't get upset. Instead, he pressed a finger to his lips. "Don't tell Mayna what I said to Iris, all right?"

I nodded timidly. "Your secret's safe with me."

He smiled slightly. "That being said, it looks like I didn't need to bother—it seems Iris was going to have to acknowledge Mayna's talent sooner or later. Perhaps I should've just stayed out of it."

"Mayna really is incredible," I agreed.

But the look in his eyes told me he desperately wanted to be there for her.

❀ ❀ ❀

THAT night, after we helped the Princess into bed, Rebecca and I left her quarters. Our shift had ended at last.

Out in the hall, we found Mayna and Sir Ray walking together. Mayna had already put Her Highness's hair into bedtime braids, and as such, her work for the day was complete. As for Sir Ray, he seemed to have finished his shift as well. My guess was that he had tracked her down so they could head home together.

"I invited Lady Iris to the castle today so I could show her how to style her new hair."

"Oh really? How did it go?" Sir Ray asked innocently.

Mayna's face lit up. "She really liked them! Every last one of them! And she told me she'd come around on her new cut, too. Apparently everyone's been giving her lots of compliments!"

"That's good to hear."

"I'm just so glad to see she's feeling better! Oh, and she told me to tell you she said hello..." She paused, frowning. "Specifically, she wanted me to tell you she was very nice to me. Is something going on with you two, or am I way off-base?"

"Can't say I know what she's talking about," Sir Ray replied casually. Clearly he was a good liar. "Anyway, I'm really glad you got Lady Iris to change her mind about her hair. I saw her walking by, actually. Her hair looks great."

"Hee hee! It really does, doesn't it?" Mayna grinned to herself cheerfully.

This smile proved infectious, and soon Sir Ray was grinning along with her. He glanced back at us and shot me a wink, as if to say, "Our little secret." I answered him with a curt nod.

Fortunately Mayna didn't notice our exchange, but Rebecca was a different story. "What was that?"

"Oh, nothing."

I wasn't about to blab to *anyone*, much less Mayna. After all, I didn't especially want to find out what would happen if I made Sir Ray angry.

Meanwhile, I envisioned Padell's soft, warm smile. Sir Ray was certainly good-looking, but he was just too *intense*...

In the end, I think fate made the right choice for both of us.

Afterword

MY name is Tsukasa Mikuni. Thank you for reading *Of Dragons and Fae: Is a Fairy Tale Ending Possible for the Princess's Hairstylist?!* It has been an honor to have my story translated from Japanese to English. Now readers outside of Japan can enjoy it, too. At least, I certainly hope you did!

So there I was, writing this story about a protagonist who works as a hairstylist. Naturally, I had a lot of trouble thinking of what hairstyles to give Mayna and Patricia. At first I thought maybe I should go with something really extravagant, like Marie Antoinette, but eventually I decided they should have hairstyles in line with modern fashion. Alas, no miniature ship models for Mayna.

Fun fact: You know in Chapter 8, when Kirion is introduced and Mayna tells the room about the most famous male hairstylist in Myulan history? That conversation was based directly on Marie Antoinette's real relationship with her stylist, Léonard Autié. He was actually a huge source of inspiration for me when writing about hairstyling.

Oh, and Patricia's curly hair is based on my own hair, so I think it's safe to say I've depicted the curly hair experience pretty accurately. It's thick and unruly and a real pain to deal with, but it helped me write this book, so for the first time in my life, I'm actually grateful I was born with it!

With my curly hair, I can't just brush it and leave the house. I have to braid it, or style it, or use careful pin placement, or straighten it, or curl it in opposite directions. *Every morning.* All my life, I've experimented with hair products and accessories, and I've even had to cut it myself. After all, Japan doesn't have a ton of curly-haired people, so a lot of professional barbers don't know how to cut it. Chances are, if I go to a salon, I'll come out looking weird.

But now I've channeled my lifelong hair struggles into this book, so I feel like I can finally let go and learn to love my natural curls. Besides, if Mayna were here, I'm sure she'd say, "You have great hair! It's so easy to style!"

Before I go, I'd like to once again extend my gratitude to all of my readers—thank you! To Cross Infinite World—thank you for translating it. A big thank you to my illustrator, YukiKana, as well as all others involved. May we meet again someday!

Of Dragons and Fae

Is a Fairy Tale Ending Possible for the Princess's Hairstylist?

LITTLE PRINCESS IN FAIRY FOREST
STORY BY: TSUBAKI TOKINO
ILLUSTRATION BY: TAKASHI KONNO
STANDALONE | OUT NOW

Join Princess Lala and Sir Gideon as they flee for their lives from the traitor who killed the royal family and wants to wed Lala! Gideon is willing to do anything to protect his princess, even if it means engaging the mighty dragons in combat! Tsubaki Tokino's fairy tale inspired Little Princess in Fairy Forest!

ANOTHER WORLD'S ZOMBIE APOCALYPSE IS NOT MY PROBLEM!
STORY BY: HARU YAYARI
ILLUSTRATION BY: FUYUKI
STANDALONE | OUT NOW

Just when I thought navigating high school was bad enough, I woke up to a rotting, post-apocalyptic world!

THE ECCENTRIC MASTER AND THE FAKE LOVER!
STORY BY: ROKA SAYUKI
ILLUSTRATION BY: ITARU
VOL. 1 OUT NOW

Yanked into another world full of dangerous magic and parasitic plants, Nichika does the one thing she can to survive: become the apprentice to an eccentric witch!

THE CHAMPIONS OF JUSTICE AND THE SUPREME RULER OF EVIL
STORY BY: KAEDE KIKYOU
ILLUSTRATION BY: TOBARI
STANDALONE | OUT NOW

Mia's a supervillain bent on world domination who lacks tact in enacting her evil schemes! Will the lazy superheroes be able to stop her?

BEAST † BLOOD
STORY BY: TSUKASA YAMAZAKI
ILLUSTRATION BY: KIYU KANAE
VOL. 1 OUT NOW

Biotech Scientist Euphemia's world suddenly gets flipped upside down when her sister hires a sexy alien mercenary to be her bodyguard!

THE CURSED PRINCESS AND THE LUCKY KNIGHT
STORY BY: UTA NARUSAWA
ILLUSTRATION BY: TAKASHI KIRIYA
STANDALONE | OUT NOW

Orphan Sonia leaves the abbey only to be haunted by her own castle! Is an arranged marriage to a knight her only salvation from the family curse?

Printed in Great Britain
by Amazon